CONTEMPORARY AMERICAN FICTION

BETWEEN C&D

Joel Rose is the coeditor of *Between C&D* magazine. His first novel, *Kill the Poor*, will be published by Atlantic Monthly Press in September of 1988. Catherine Texier, the other coeditor of *Between C&D* magazine, is the author of the novel *Love Me Tender*, which is available from Penguin.

BETWEEN C&D

New Writing from the Lower East Side Fiction Magazine

Edited by

JOEL ROSE
and
CATHERINE TEXIER

PENGUIN BOOKS

Sex
Drugs
Violence
Danger
Computers

PENGUIN BOOKS
Published by the Penguin Group
Viking Penguin Inc., 40 West 23rd Street,
New York, New York 10010, U.S.A.
Penguin Books Ltd, 27 Wrights Lane,
London W8 5TZ, England
Penguin Books Australia Ltd, Ringwood,
Victoria, Australia
Penguin Books Canada Ltd, 2801 John Street,
Markham, Ontario, Canada L3R 1B4
Penguin Books (N.Z.) Ltd, 182–190 Wairau Road,
Auckland 10, New Zealand

Penguin Books Ltd, Registered Offices:
Harmondsworth, Middlesex, England

First published in Penguin Books 1988
Published simultaneously in Canada

All the selections in this collection first appeared in issues of *Between C&D*.

"Male" by Kathy Acker. Reprinted by permission of Curtis Brown Associates Ltd.
Copyright © 1987 by Kathy Acker.
"Case History #179: Tina" by Tama Janowitz. Copyright © 1987 by Tama Janowitz.
"I Am Candy Jones" by Gary Indiana. © 1985 by Gary Indiana.
"Dead Talk" by Lynne Tillman. © Lynne Tillman 1986.
"Oak" by Barry Yourgrau. Copyright Barry Yourgrau; from *Wearing Dad's Head*,
Peregrine Smith Books, Salt Lake City, 1987.
"The Woman in the Shadows" by Roberta Allen. © Roberta Allen 1987.

LIBRARY OF CONGRESS CATALOGING IN PUBLICATION DATA
Between C&D : new writing from the Lower East Side fiction magazine
/ edited by Joel Rose and Catherine Texier.
p. cm.—(Contemporary American fiction)
ISBN 0 14 01.0570 0
1. American fiction—20th century. 2. American fiction—New York
(N.Y.) 3. Lower East Side (New York, N.Y.)—Fiction. 4. New York
(N.Y.)—Fiction. I. Rose, Joel. II. Texier, Catherine.
III. Lower East Side fiction magazine. IV. Title: Between C and D.
V. Series.
PS659.B44 1988
813'.01'089747—dc19   87-24386
                                                                CIP

Printed in the United States of America by
R. R. Donnelley & Sons Company, Harrisonburg, Virginia
Set in Century Expanded
Designed by Francesca Belanger

To Céline

*With special thanks to David Berger,
the Coordinating Council of Literary Magazines,
the New York State Council of the Arts,
and Epson America.*

CONTENTS

INTRODUCTION

When we first began *Between C&D* in the winter of 1983/84, there were already magazines publishing "new fiction" in New York City: there were *Bomb*, *Red Tape*, *Benzene*, and *Top Stories*, for instance. But, apart from *Top Stories*, which publishes fiction in chapbook form, one writer apiece, most of the Downtown publications which included fiction mixed short stories with poetry, articles and essays, or had a strong visual-art slant, sandwiching a fiction quickie between pages and pages of art or photography.

If you were a writer living in Manhattan in the early eighties and didn't feel any affinity for the school of "dirty realism" or weren't writing "sensitive" narration teeming with believable characters a reader could care for throughout the length of a novel, you were left high and dry on the Downtown shore. *Between C&D* offered an exclusive forum for these writers, both established and emerging, whose voices were not being heard in the usual gamut of conventional literary magazines.

The combination of our high-tech look—the computer printout, the fanfold paper, the dot-matrix print type—in conjunction with handmade art by East Village (or Downtown) artists on the front and back covers, and the zip-lock plastic bag binding, along with, needless to say, the featured "new writing," immediately attracted both readers and writers, from New York City and elsewhere. Our print run, originally planned to be no more than seventy-five per issue, quickly increased to six hundred copies per printing: a small circulation, compared to big "little" magazines, but six hundred is our absolute maximum, due to the inordinate amount of time it takes to make each copy, every one of them printed on our home computer printers. We have published thirteen issues at this point. Each has sold out. We have a constant demand for back issues, and print them from our computer floppy disks; a number of people and institutions (the Whitney Museum, the Museum of Modern Art, the New Museum of Contemporary Art, for example) evidently enjoy collecting them.

The twenty-five writers we are including in this anthology represent some of the strongest voices we have published in the magazine over our four years' existence. They are not, by any means, the *only* strong voices we have published, but they best represent the spirit of the magazine: gritty, urban, sometimes ironic, sometimes gutsy, erotic, violent, or deadpan, unsentimental rather than "sensitive" or "psychological," playing with form but clearly narrative by intention. A few of these writers are already well established, e.g., Kathy Acker, Tama Janowitz, and Barry Yourgrau, albeit in very different literary circles. A number of others recently have had first novels or collections of short stories published with major publishers, including Lynne Tillman, Susan Daitch, Patrick McGrath, and Catherine Texier, or with small presses, such as Gary Indiana and Roberta Allen; others have novels forthcoming, such as Dennis Cooper and Joel Rose.

The range of writing is wide, in no way subscribing to any single strain, movement or dictate: from Lisa Blaushild's minimalist irony, to Gary Indiana's cynical sarcasm, to Dennis Cooper's super-hard-boiled nihilistic fiction; from Lynne Tillman's disarmingly frank prose, to Darius James' provocative black black humor, to David Wojnarowicz' breathless monologues; from Peter Cherches' absurdist mini-tales, to Patrick McGrath's baroque gothic prose, to Kathy Acker's maximalist grab bag of genres and plagiarized styles.

This is not writing-school writing (even though a few of the writers have attended them: Joel Rose has an MFA from Columbia University, Rick Henry earned his MFA from Bowling Green State, and Pete Cherches and Lisa Blaushild have also gone through the mill); this may partly explain why the styles vary to such an extent. There can be similarities between or, rather, echoes among styles, but each writer has a highly individualized voice.

Between C&D doesn't represent a school of writing nor a literary movement. Maybe a case could be made for a geographical connection: a number of writers live on the Lower East Side of Manhattan, and most of them live in large cities (ranging from LA to London). Or for a common inheritance: they owe more to Burroughs, Miller, Genet or Céline or even to Barthes and Foucault or J.G Ballard, than they do to Updike or Cheever. In the classic tradition of the avant-garde, they use sex, violence, shock value, parody, cynicism, irony, and black humor to attack the complacency of the established literature and its middle-class values.

In any case, these writers are closer to urban archaeologists than to landscape artists or campus sociologists, and regardless of their backgrounds, they choose to explore the underside of life—the frontier where the urban fabric is wearing thin and splitting open.

What these writers share is a common passion for exploring the limits of fiction in this the late twentieth century and a rebelliousness against the established order of traditional narrative. You won't find any middle-class family dramas or cute college tales in these stories. Nor are there coy, slickly portrayed vignettes of modern life. The work is sometimes shocking in its frank sexuality or violence, in its absence of sentimentality, in the deliberate sketchiness of the characters. And even the most polished stories have a gritty, jagged edge, as they attempt to break through the slick surface and hypocrisy of smooth, airtight contemporary fiction, desperately seeking to expose what lies beneath the cracks.

Joel Rose/Catherine Texier
Editors
Between C&D
New York City
July 1987

BETWEEN C&D

DAVID WOJNAROWICZ

Self Portrait
in Twenty-three Rounds

So my heritage is a calculated fuck on some faraway sunfilled bed
while the curtains are being sucked in and out of an open window
by a passing breeze. I'd be lying if I were to tell you I could
remember the smell of sweat as I hadnt even been born yet.
Conceptions just a shot in the dark. I'm supposed to be dead right
now but I just woke up this dingo motherfucker having hit me
across the head with a slab of marble that instead of splitting my
head open laid a neat sliver of eyeglass lens through the bullseye
center of my left eye. We were coming through this four and a
half day torture of little or no sleep. Thats the breaks: we were
staying at this one drag queens house but her man did her wrong
by being seen by some other queen with a vicious tongue in a
darkened lot on the westside fucking some cute little puertorican
boy in the face and when me and my buddy knocked on the door
to try and get a mattress to lay down on she sent a bullet through
the door thinking it was her man—after three days of no sleep
and maybe a couple of stolen donuts my eyes start separating in
terms of movement: one goes left and one goes right and after four
days sitting on some stoop on a sidestreet head cradled in my arms
seeing four hours of pairs of legs walking by too much traffic noise

and junkies trying to rip us off and the sunlight so hot this is a newyork summer I feel my brains slowly coming to a boil in whatever red blue liquid the brains float in and looking down the street or walking around I begin to see large rats the size of shoeboxes; ya see them just outa the corner of your eyes, in the outer sphere of sight and when ya turn sharp to look at them theyve just disappeared around the corner or down a subway steps and I'm so sick my gums start bleedin everytime I breathe and after the fifth day I start seeing what looks like the limbs of small kids, arms and legs in the mouths of these rats and no screaming mommies or daddies to lend proof to the image and late last night me and my buddy were walking around with two meat cleavers we stole from Macy's gourmet section stuck in between our belts and dry skin lookin for someone to mug and some queer on the uppereast side tried to pick us up but my buddys meat cleaver dropped out the back of his pants just as the guy was opening the door to his building and clang clangalang the guy went apeshit his screams bouncing through the night off half a million windows of surrounding apartments we ran thirty blocks till we felt safe. Some nights we had so much hate for the world and each other all these stupid dreams of finding his fosterparents who he tried poisoning with a box of rat poison when they let him out of the attic after keeping him locked in there for a month and a half after all dear its summer vacation and no one will miss you heres a couple jugs of springwater and cereal don't eat it all at once we're off on a holiday after all its better this than we return you to that nasty kids home. His parents had sharp tastebuds and my buddy spent eight years in some jail for the criminally insane even though he was just a minor. Somehow though he had this idea to find his folks and scam lots of cash off them so we could start a new life. Some nights we'd walk seven or eight hundred blocks practically the whole island of manhattan crisscrossing east and west north and south each on opposite sides of the streets picking up every wino bottle we found and throwing it ten feet into the air so it crash exploded a couple of inches away from the others feet—on nights that called for it every pane of glass in every phone booth from here to southstreet would dissolve in a shower of light. We slept good after a night of this in some abandoned car boiler room rooftop or lonely drag queens palace.

If I were to leave this country and never come back or see it again in films or sleep I would still remember a number of different things that sift back in some kind of tidal motion. I remember when I was eight years old I would crawl out the window of my apartment seven stories above the ground and hold on to the ledge with ten scrawny fingers and lower myself out above the sea of cars burning up eighth avenue and hang there like a stupid motherfucker for five minutes at a time testing my own strength dangling I liked the rough texture of the bricks against the tip of my sneakers and when I got tired I'd haul myself back in for a few minutes rest and then climb back out testing testing testing how do I control this how much control do I have how much strength do I have waking up with a mouthful of soot sleeping on these shitty birdfilled rooftops waking up to hardassed sunlight burning the tops of my eyes and I aint had much to eat in three days except for the steak we stole from A&P and cooked in some bum kitchen down the lower east side the workers were friendly to us that way and we looked clean compared to the others and really I had dirt scabs behind my ears I hadnt washed in months but once in a while in the mens room of a horn and hardarts on forty second street in between standing around hustling for some red eyed bastard with pink face and a wallet fulla singles to come up behind me and pinch my ass murmuring something about good times and good times for me was just one fucking night of solid sleep which was impossible I mean the boiler room of some highrise the pipes would start clanking and hissing like machine pistons putting together a tunnel under the river from here to jersey and its only the morning 6 AM heat piping in to all those people up above our heads and I'm looking like one of them refugees in the back of life magazine only no care packages for me they give me some tickets up at the salvation army for three meals at a soup kitchen where ya get a bowl of mucus water and sip at rotten potatoes while some guy down the table is losing his eye into his soup he didnt move fast enough on the line and some fucked up wino they hired as guard popped him in the eye with a bottle and I'm so lacking in those lovely vitamins they put in wonderbread and real family meals that when I puff one drag off my cigarette blood pours out between my teeth sopping into the nonfilter and that buddy of mine complains that he won't smoke it after me and in the horn and hardarts theres a table full of deaf mutes and theyre the loudest people in the joint one of them seventy years old takes me to a nearby hotel once a month when his disability check comes in and he has me lay down on my belly and he dry humps me harder and harder and his dick is soft and banging against my ass and his arm is mashing my little face up as he goes through his routine of pretending to come and starts hollering the way only a deaf mute can holler sounds like donkeys braying when snakes come around but somehow in the midst of all that I love him maybe its the way he returns to his table of friends in the cafeteria a smile busted across his face and I'm the one with the secret and twenty dollars in my pocket and then theres the fetishist who one time years ago picked me up and told me this story of how he used to be in the one platoon in fort dix where they shoved all the idiots and illiterates and poor bastards that thought kinda slow and the ones with speeth spitch speeeeeeech impediments that means ya talk funny he said and I nodded one of my silent yes's that I'd give as conversation to anyone with a tongue in those days and every sunday morning this sadistic sonuvabitch of a sergeant would come into the barracks and make the guys come out one by one and attempt to publicly read the sunday funnies blondie and dagwood and beetlebailey and dondi with his stupid morals I was glad when some little delinquent punched his face in one sunday and he had a shiner three sundays in a row in full color till the strip couldnt get anymore mileage out of it and some cop busted the delinquent and put him back in the reform school he escaped from and all the while these poor slobs are trying to read even one line the sergeant is saying lookit this stupid sonuvabitch how the fuck do you expect to serve this country of yours and you cant even read to save your ass and he'd run around the barracks smacking all the guys in the head one after the other and make them force them to laugh at this guy tryin to read until it was the next guys turn and when we got to his place there was three cats pissing all over the joint crusty brown cans of opened cat food littering the floor window open so they could leave by the fire escape and he had this thing for rubber he'd dress me up in this sergeant outfit but with a pair of rubber sneakers that they made only during world war two when it was important to do that I guess canvas was a material they needed for the war effort or something and anyway so he would have me put on these pure rubber sneakers and the sergeant's outfit and then a rubber trenchcoat and then he'd put on this rubber over his dick and he had another rubber sneaker that he'd grease up and he would start fucking the rubber sneaker while on his belly and I'd have to shove my sneakers sole against his face and tell him to lick the dirt off the bottom of them and all the while cursing at him telling how stupid he was a fuckin dingo stupid dog aint worth catfood whered you get your fuckin brains surprised they even let ya past the m.p.'s on the front gate oughta call in the trucks and have you carted off to some idiot farm and whered you get your brains whered you get your brains and when he came into his rubber inside the rubber sneaker he'd roll over all summer sweaty and say oh that was a good load musta ate some eggs today and I'm already removin my uniform and he says he loves the way my skeleton moves underneath my skin when I bend over to retrieve one of my socks.

LISA BLAUSHILD

Witness

I admit it, I don't do shit.

I never do.

I adopt a "wait and see" attitude.

Most of the time these things just go away by themselves. Why jump to unnecessary conclusions?

I sit up in bed. I buff my nails. I try to guess where those ear-piercing screams are coming from. The garden below my window? The park? The TV next door? It's fun to play detective.

A woman getting bludgeoned to death and a cat in heat sound remarkably similar.

It's easy to be fooled.

Rooftop slaying or children playing?

Most people don't realize dialing 911 costs 50 cents. Let the neighbors call.

Probably nothing more than some slut fucking.

I pick up the receiver, I put it down again.

In the park I hold the *Times* in front of my face. What is that couple doing over there? Are they struggling or *dancing?* Vicious assault or April Fool's Day gag?

It's not polite to stare.

I never take a stand until I've heard both sides of a story.

She runs away, he catches up, pins her to the ground, a knife to her throat. I glance at my watch, I've got to be going.

Nobody likes a busybody.

I pull my hat down over my face and walk toward the nearest exit. Only cowards run.

Victim of rape or eager and willing? Hey I'm not one to spoil somebody else's party.

One foot in front of the other. That's how I make tracks.

The bitch probably deserved it.

Actual cries for help or attention-seeking publicity hound?

I shout out the window, Okay, I heard you the first time! Would you shut up already? I've got to get some shut-eye or I'm going to look like shit tomorrow.

To avoid stray bullets I stay close to the floor. Reach up, slam the window shut.

What ever happened to those silent killers of yesteryear? They'd do their job swiftly and efficiently, and the rest of us still got a full night's sleep.

She sent him mixed signals. She wanted it, she didn't want it. The cockteaser.

Mugging in progress or "Trick or Treat" time?

The school bully offered me $1.00 to keep my mouth shut after I spotted him setting fire to the girl's locker room. Pal, I said, make it $1.50 and you've got yourself a deal.

"Officer, it was impossible to tell what he looked like with that stocking mask on."

"Which way did he go?" Like the scarecrow, I wrap my arms around myself and point in opposite directions.

Manslaughter or fraternity initiation rite?

They're probably just filming another episode of *The Equalizer*.

I live above a crack factory. They don't bother me, I don't bother them. I pound on the wall, they turn their stereo down. We respect each other's privacy.

Nobody likes a tattletale.

So he slaps her around a little.

I say to the guy reading the newspaper next to me, Do you see what I see? He says, Do you see what *I* see? We shudder. Team-work.

We agree. Serves her right for taking a walk so late at night in a changing neighborhood.

He should have given him his wallet the first time he asked.

Sometimes you get what's coming to you.

A hit-and-run. I watched a black sedan speed away in a cloud of dust. Sorry officer, I said, I had the license plate memorized, couldn't find a pen, then I forgot it.

Preppie murder or was she "hurting" him?

Check out what she's wearing! The whore.

From a safe distance I size up the assailant. Isn't it the thought that counts?

I could go to a lot of trouble for nothing. What if my photograph doesn't get in the paper? The mayor doesn't praise my heroism?

Rule: I never intervene if I'm on my way to the office. I'd mess up my suit.

Six of *them* against one of *me*? I'm not crazy!

What, with my own bare hands?

He could have a gun.

I stumble upon a body. Critically wounded as a result of multiple stab wounds or homeless bum taking a nap? Tiptoe away.

They could say I did it. A case of mistaken identity. It's uncanny the way the police sketch looks exactly like me. They'll lock me up, throw away the key.

In the morning a cardboard figure lay in the grass where the girl had been murdered. The neighbors and I looked at each other with surprise, "I thought *you* called."

Don't blame us. Blame the system.

We're good people. We're a community. We donate money to the Wildlife Preservation Fund each year. We *care*.

Nothing like this has ever happened in our neck of the woods before.

What a shame. She was such a lovely girl.

Oh well, that's life in the big city.

That's par for the course.

If you can't stand the heat get out of the kitchen.

A cop at my door. He asks me questions. I cut him short. Officer, I say, I'm one of those lucky people who can sleep through anything.

RICK HENRY

Subject:
Petri Ganton

INTEROFFICE MEMO

To: Chief   Date: August 12, 1982
From: Detective Waser

As you have requested, I have pulled the files on Petri Ganton and have summarized all pertinent information.

1. On Oct. 14, 1969 Petri Ganton was found dead in his apartment at 245 Ingles St. by his landlady. He had no identification, nor was his identity confirmed.

2. The cause of death was heart failure due to the poison strophanthin.

3. He was found with an envelope in his hand. The envelope was empty, and addressed to Walkside Publishing House.

4. Traces of strophanthin were found in the glue on the envelope.

5. Walkside had no knowledge of Ganton. No one recognized his photograph.

6. The case was closed June 23, 1975. It was listed as Probable Suicide.

Two days ago, we received *Notes* in the mail. There was no return address on the envelope, nor was there an accompanying letter. Interesting things to note:

1. It is apparently the editor's notes about a novel written by Ganton.

2. The entire first page is charred, as are the edges of the rest of the pages. It is possible the novel was burned.

3. Preliminary reports show that the paper the text is printed on is ten to fifteen years old. Reports also show that the charring is about ten years old.

4. Note that the author of the notes is Andrew Cammeron, the date is 1969, and the publisher is Walkside. I have gone over the publishing lists from 1967 to the present and have found no such book listed—either by the title *Crocodile*, or by the author Petri Ganton. Walkside has no record of an editor by the name of Andrew Cammeron.

From our files:

August 28, 1967. Ganton charged with harassment by Pete Domain. Officers were dispatched to bring Ganton in, but his apartment was empty, his whereabouts unknown.

July 15, 1968. Graham Wilson charged Ganton with aggravated assault. Officers charged Wilson with disorderly conduct. Charges were dropped against Wilson. Officers were dispatched to bring Ganton in, but he was not found.

Both cases were closed on Oct. 14, 1969 when Ganton's body was found.

From FBI files:

Note the contradictions:

1. FBI description does not match the body found.

2. Ganton's draft status was 4F.

3. Ganton was known to have had a homosexual affair with Pete Domain from July 1966 to March 1967.

4. The FBI was tipped on several occasions that Ganton was both a drug dealer and a political activist. The FBI investigated the charges and found them to be untrue.

NOTES

1. The whole book purports to be an exposé and is based largely on fact; however, Ganton has only given us the initials (for the most part) of the people involved and sometimes these do not match the real names of those he indicates. And the information he provides is often not true. For instance, Ganton admits to sleeping with the wife of a local official in chapter ten and gives her initials as O.F. Given the rest of the information, we can safely assume that the identity of the official is Remy Stuart, mayor of Palo Alto. But at the time, his wife, Augusta Stuart, was a visiting professor at an eastern university. Ganton is known not to have left the state in the entire three year period the book covers, so the information is highly suspect. What we have here is a portrait of a paranoid. The title, *Crocodile*, supports this reading. The title comes from a quote by Phaedrus, Ganton's favorite, and he quoted it to anyone who would listen: "It is said that dogs drink from the Nile running, lest a crocodile should seize them." Ganton surely thought himself to be one of the dogs, though specifically who or what agency was the crocodile is wide open. He certainly was on the run, changing residences no less than fifteen times in three years. He may, however, have considered himself the crocodile as he wrote the book, seizing the dogs that hounded his every step.

2. The address of the apartment Ganton says he moved into, as well as all the following addresses, does not exist. From the descriptions, it can be assumed that

1

all the moves were within a three mile radius and that he lived in the area of Haight-Ashbury.

3. The cause of this second move is not likely to be due to his receiving his draft notice. He was twenty years old at the time, and had been enrolled at a state university. He dropped out and probably made the move to San Francisco to avoid being called up for service as his student deferment would have been void. The second move cannot therefore be explained, unless for the same reasons as his next move, three months later, when he suspected he was being followed by the FBI. The description of the man fits that interpretation.

4. The stories he submitted to the publisher were hack work. He says he received the rejection through the mail. In actuality, he visited the publishing house on five occasions in three weeks. The last two times he had to be forcibly removed by the security guard. It was about this time he began *Crocodile*.

5. No editor at the publishing house ever went near the Acid Tests. It can be assumed that Ganton was a frequent visitor. His description is vivid and verified by all known accounts.

6. The preceding chapter shows Ganton's growing involvement with drugs, not the editor he allegedly follows. The disjointed nature of the prose, the frequent use of street names for various substances and the detailed accounts of the processes by which they are consumed show an insider's view. It is unreasonable

2

to assume a witness of the events could know of the effects of the various combinations.

7. Ganton indicates that A.C.'s wife is seeing someone else and provides a detailed description of the person. In actuality, he mailed out several letters to people at the publishing house. All were the same, words formed by cutting out letters from newspapers and magazines. One of the letters reads as follows:

i eat your wife Daily 1 pm At The Lounge et tu

There is no Lounge Et Tu within a fifty mile radius of San Francisco.

8. The three moves described here are unexplained. It is about this time that Ganton purchases black shoes, a dark suit and sunglasses, though he makes no mention of it in the text. It is probable that when he speaks of seeing a government man right outside his window, he is really seeing himself in the mirror.

9. *The Grinders*, *Shake a Fanny*, and *Female Pilot in a Cockpit* are all 16mm pornography films. "Suede Belinda" is the brand name of a rubber doll (in this case covered with leather) used by some for sexual

3

satisfaction. "Kind of Sweet" is the brand name of panties that have an edible crotch, usually made of some sort of candy, but can be flavored with anything the customer desires. In this case, it is reasonable to assume it was the candy crotch. Again, his detailed knowledge of the products indicates he was involved in their use, not the person he allegedly followed into the adult bookstore.

10. P.D. (Pete Domain) was a local poet, not a screen-mittee on UnAmerican Activities for allegedly making a pass at a government official.

11. It is probable that there are two men follow-ing Ganton here. The quick changes in clothing come too fast and are not standard procedure for the FBI. The second man was probably a drug dealer of some sort. Just before Ganton moved in with Pete Domain, he cheated several dealers. Their identities are un-known.

12. Ganton could not possibly have seen what he says he saw from his window. His view was of the kitchen. The bedroom had a window that faced in the opposite direction. That he entered the building disguised as an electrician is unlikely. The building had very tight security. It is also improbable that he even rented out the apartment across the street from which he did his spying. The rent in the district was well over $400 a month. Ganton had no known income and was still living comfortably with Domain.

4

13. Ganton says he moved out on Pete because he thought he was being followed. Pete actually threw him out, unable to tolerate the drug habit Ganton had.

14. Ganton's return visits to the Domain apartment were not as peaceful as he would have us believe. Domain lodged a complaint with the police at this time, charging Ganton with harassment. Police were unable to locate him.

15. G.P. (Ginny Peters) was 16 when they met, not 23.

16. The envelope passed from A.C. to the writer and contained an advance. It was not a bribe passed from the writer to A.C., as Ganton says.

17. Domain was not carrying a torch for Ganton. He had, in fact, already found someone else to move in with (R.T. being Graham Wilson, drummer for the band Jump Suite).

18. This whole chapter is puzzling. There is no record of anyone in the San Francisco area from 1965–8 bearing the name Gary Jorzen nor was his death ever reported to the police. This is the one time where Ganton gives us a full name. Domain died around this time and the circumstances surrounding his death were suspicious. Police listed it as probable suicide, the cause: heart failure due to the poison strophanthin. Strophanthin is derived from a group of plants of the *Strophanus* genus which are native to tropical climates—specifically Asia and Africa. In fact, strophanthin has been used by natives in Africa as an arrow poison.

5

There have been five reported cases of death by strophanthin in the United States. Two of them were reported in Florida, one in 1942, and the other in 1957.
Both cases remain a mystery to the police. Three more
cases were reported in New Orleans in 1966 when
police found three members of the underworld dead
in a restaurant. Local papers picked up on the case
but the national news services did not. How Ganton
knew of the poison is unknown.

19. Ganton reports three people following him now.
One fits the description of Graham Wilson.

20. A confusing chapter. Ganton appears to have assumed three disguises, each corresponding to the people he suspects of following him. Why he would assume
these poses as he follows A.C. is unknown.

21. Details of the orgy he allegedly witnesses are
physically impossible. The prose begins to break down
again, indicating his dependence on drugs. Where he
gets them is unknown, the dealers are still looking for
him and it is unlikely they would supply him with anything. The whole scene is probably an hallucination.

22. Imagery here indicates that Ganton and Ginny Peters were indeed married in a Free Love ceremony.
Witnesses verify this account.

23. That Ganton threw Ginny out because she was a
government agent is unlikely. She did in fact leave him
during another Acid Test, escorted by six members of
a motorcycle gang. She was overheard as saying that
Ganton was into perversions and that didn't sit well
with her. This is likely a lie, not that Ganton was into

6

perversions, but that they didn't sit well with her. She became the woman of all six men for a time, before she left the country. She is now being sought by the CIA in connection with sabotage, the recent explosion at a power plant in Nicaragua and several counts of gun running in El Salvador. That Ganton followed Ginny out of the Test and was severely beaten is probably true, despite the fact that local hospitals have no record of treating him for such wounds as he received.

24. Here marks the end of the first manuscript of *Crocodile*.

25. His fears that the publishing house would steal the manuscript are evidenced by his visit with the lawyer. The lawyer is in no way connected with the publishing house as Ganton suggests.

26. Description is again of Graham Wilson. Wilson was picked up by the police and charged with disorderly conduct. Wilson filed a complaint against Ganton, charging him with aggravated assault. Police were unable to locate him.

27. Correspondence with the publishing house at this time was actually a series of threat letters. The publishers reported these to the police.

28. The increased paranoia on the part of Ganton is evidenced by the length he goes to in describing the number of people following him.

29. Here marks the end of the text. That it stops in mid-sentence is strange, especially since he mailed it to the publishing house that way. The house received

7

the manuscript through the mail on October 15th. It was postmarked the 12th. Ganton was found dead in his apartment by his landlady on the 14th—his body already decomposing. After a cursory investigation, the police deemed his death suicide, caused by strophanthin. Three weeks later, the house decided to publish the work. The text is as Ganton submitted it, complete with misspellings. The editors feel that these notes should accompany the text in the interest of clarity.

Andrew Cammeron
Editor
Walkside Publishing House
1969

8

KATHY ACKER

Male

From the novel *Empire of the Senseless*

As long as I can remember, I have wanted to be a pirate. As long as I can remember, I have wanted to sail the navy seas. As long as I can remember wanting, I have wanted to slaughter other humans and to watch the emerging of their blood.

Insofar as I know myself I don't know either the origin or the cause of my wants.

It was a dark night for pirates.

Winter had approached all of us on the ship. One night whose beginning was death, three pirates squatting on the deck just like fat cunts or pigs held a consultation which lingered, like death, without becoming anything else. For one human they had taken during their last battle remained bound and gagged near the bowsprit. Their discussion became more confused, then too confused, at least for the victim who could still hear; the pirates had become increasingly drunk. A fat slob waddled over to the victim who was a child and raped her again.

She didn't struggle as the other two did the same.

"Afterwards I'd like to do it to you," the first pirate turned to the second pirate.

"No. I'm younger than you so it's possible for me to have a child. I don't want one. Just cause it's safe for you . . ."

"Not if I do it in your asshole. In your asshole you're safe."

"Just stop what you're doing. Above all I don't want to be pregnant!"

"You don't believe me. You don't trust . . ."

"No." The second one explained: "Why should I trust you? You tell me why I should trust you. You tell me why I should trust you who can't get pregnant not to make me pregnant."

The third pirate came in his pants. A round stain showed.

"Don't you believe I can fuck you and not make babies?"

Used to protecting his virginity like a girl, the youngest of the pirates capitulated. "If you let me alone I'll let you do it tonight. But you've got to promise you won't tell anyone."

Fatty replied "I promise" since he never meant anything by these words. "But you're going to spread yourself for me now. Otherwise I want that thin trigger that thin cock you're showing me so much, I'll cut off your head to get at it." Among themselves, also, pirates're murderous. "But after I come when you're dead, you can do whatever you want."

Fatty dove in, ground and pounded his cock up into the so tight it was almost impenetrable asshole. He pound and ground until the brat started wiggling; then thrust hard. Thrust fast. Living backbone. Jewel at top of hole. The asshole opened involuntarily. The kid screeched like nerves. After a while the kid felt Fatty become still. After a few more minutes he asked Fatty if he had come.

"Shut up. Shut. Up." As it dropped out the final bit of sperm inflamed the top of his cockhole.

Barely mumbling "Now it's time for me now it's time for what I want," the pirate who had just been fucked bent over the child tightly bound in ropes, already raped. His hands reached for her breasts. While sperm which resembled mutilated oysters dropped out of his asshole, he touched the breasts.

The three pirates turned away from the child. They went back to their work of gnawing and gorging themselves on Nestle's almonds, Cadbury chocolates flakes, barbecued tortilla chips, green beans, toffeed vanilla, Lucozade, and Mars bars. They guzzled down can after can of swill.

The Captain, me, walked on deck. "What a group of pigs! Didn't your teachers in all the nice boarding schools you went to, which you never talk about, teach you about nutrition?"

"This ship isn't a public school," Fatty blurted out through showers of Coca-Cola mixed with beer. "This shit is a pirate ship. And this is a philanthropic association."

"Sure," Captain Thivai, me, sneered. "I'm a sweet socialist government so I'm paying you to sit on your asses in the sun and get suntanned just so that you are so happy you won't revolt against my economic fascism."

Fatty dared to oppose me. "No way. This ship is our philanthropic association, our place of safety, our baby crib. Since they have enough dough to be our charity donors, all the people outside it, all the people outside us here, are our enemies.

"Since we live on this ship, we're orphans. Orphans are dumb and stupid." Fatty was epileptic. "Since we're stupid, we don't know how to conduct ourselves in decent (monied) society and we kill people for no reason.

"Historically, weren't some of the most violent political murderers," the punk added, "aristocrats?"

"Do all of you have parents?" I asked my crew. I was astounded. "Do you generally come from good backgrounds?"

"How can I answer a generality? So how can I answer any question?" Fatty obviously came from a superior background.

"Do you," pointing my finger at the youngest therefore the weakest of the lot, "do you, personally, have parents?"

"I don't have no parents."

"Me neither."

"Him also?"

"No one."

"None."

"No one has nothing anymore."

"Then who'd you come out of and where d'you come from?" I wasn't going to be fooled by the scum.

"That's our business. Each one of us."

The English pirate answered. "We're not used to discussing private affairs. It's not your business on whom we piss."

I had to agree with the English, for it was necessary for me to trust my crew about whom I knew nothing except that they were not the scum of the earth, they were the scum of the now scum-filled seas.

And the next day, when the ship stopped near a shore on which a bordello was stretching out its claws, I jumped ship. A cock cried on the top of the hill. Roosters' red crests jumped through the weighted-down grasses. A guard and his heavy gun descended. I hid from him.

Where there were buildings, huge trees had showered dew on to their red roofs. My fear dried up my throat. My hands lay over my stomach for protection.

The sun . . .

Fear disintegrated my throat . . .

Stunned . . .

I woke. I was no longer free. Words woke me. "It's me, Xaintrilles. This afternoon the General Staff'll interrogate you. Good luck 'n all that. I'm leaving for Ait Saada."

I didn't speak.

Xaintrilles squatted down on his haunches and looked at the bars. He saw a young man spread flat on the floor, still, his knees apart, a sackcloth jacket over only part of his stomach. "Thivai, aren't you listening to me? Maybe you can't hear anymore?"

I recognized despair enough to open my senses only inside me. Lice gnawed my cropped head. Xaintrilles carried this body inside, chafed hands and knees.

In the deep river firemen and convoy soldiers washed themselves. Mud scintillated around the decaying bathhouse.

I lovingly rubbed my skull, the light wounds the hairchopper had made. "Shave me. To the flesh," I said.

The gentle haircutter, as soon as his officer had left, positioned the straight razor at the front of the forehead. "Thivai, I can't. There's not enough left."

Upon returning, the officer looked at the prisoner and ordered the barber to shave him totally.

I smiled, I lowered my head, the barber trembled, my flesh peeled off my head and the tip of my ear, the officer by his red leather boot crushed my shoeless foot; the cutter wiped his fingers on the linen knotted around my neck. Then he went back to his cutting. My hairs dropped off like flies. As they were cut, they brushed by the ears, the holes of the nostrils, caught in the eyebrows, mommy, I only want the hairdresser to cut off a lock of hair, my matchstick, mommy's sitting in the armchair, mommy's holding my knee, mommy's picking up a magazine, mommy puts it on her knees. Veronique's behind the mirror. Veronique stands upright. Then the hairdresser pushes her down while Veronique makes signs which the mirror reflects. The cut hairs brush past the beehive I've hidden in my shirt; mommy leaves, forgetting her purse. She walks through the rain along the river. Am I dreaming? The haircutter looks around him, he puts his hand on the hot flannel of my pants, his hand climbs up my thigh, I look at Veronique, it's she who's raping me it's she who's touching me, mommy's screaming out loud and crying in the rain.

Dock workers drag barbed-wire sheets through the slush. Mommy bites her soaked scarf. The haircutter's hand sinks between my knees; again I push it away; his other hand travels down my stomach; my knees hit the marble washbasin which nevertheless maintains its balance; the haircutter's hand rests openly on my obviously palpitating stomach. The hairdresser looks behind him.

Under the door, mommy's drying her shoes. She enters the room. Night falls. Her wet hands hold my small ones, I fall into the armchair; mommy pays the hairdresser; he presses me against the door.

Mommy drags me out, down black streets until we reach the river. The dock workers're trying to warm themselves by standing as close as possible to a fire made out of charcoal dust. Mommy, holding me in her arms, jumps into the thicker mist. She mounts the jetty and runs over the rocks. Snow is covering the rocks. I try to writhe myself away, but she's pressing me into her hips. So I bite her hand, while a tugboat whose bright port deadlights are throwing glimmers on a black oily sea, moves down the estuary; mommy throws herself, . . . , I bite her hand, as her arms let go, I fall down the rocks, rolling down the rocks, mommy falls into the sea, (my mother's suicide), the foam finds and recovers her, I twist my body round toward the rocks. There a wave carries my mother's head. Her palms slide along a sleek, slightly glittering rock. The tugboat bears the other way, then stops; a sailor runs on to a bridge; he unfastens a yawl, runs back on board; they row toward the jetty. Between the clouds the stars're shining. My head's bathing in a small abandoned puddle. A sailor jumps onto the jetty, lifts me in his strong arms, up, strokes my forehead and left cheek. The other sailors ship their oars and, lifting up my mother's body, bear it over a huge flat rock. The sailor puts me to bed. From the tip of the tent's main peg a lantern was barely balancing. My blood flowed into my hands. The sailors telephoned, held my hands in theirs, covered my face. They tore the khaki posters and bills open . . .

After the jeeps and the lorries left, wounded on the forehead now by the rising sun, I placed my sackcloth jacket over my face. The rest was naked. The flies in the toilet and the winepress the soldiers had for their own convenience were gnawing at the barrier wires' edges; they darted forward, leapt over my cock, sunk into the mop of hair below, skirted over the curly locks, so I trembled, opened my thighs. The morning breeze cooled down the thighs and the sexual mass. The flies stole . . .

Again Veronique tosses her hair behind her; I take hold of this hair and throw my face into it; Veronique turns around and places my head in her hands:

"Xaintrilles wet-kissed me in the garden."

I throw my arms around her waist, then I eat at her mouth; revolving her thighs rub and press themselves against my stomach;

though she's pushing back my arms, I kiss her eyelids; her hand rubs my back my waist; her eyelids taste of mud; the sweat wets my opened shirt.

As soon as she laughs, I turn her over under me on the armchair.

The wind bangs the books on the table shut. My hand burrows like a mole in her clothes. Over a teat. Trembles. Under my hand the teat is hot. I stroke the other teat. With the second hand I unhook the dress. And tongue the teat's tip. "And me," she pants. She crushes my mouth by her breast. Wide open the windows look over the park. Xaintrilles walks through the thick grass, his gun erect.

"Don't be so hard," he tells me. "You're breaking my legs."

I crawl over him. Sirens stain the distance.

Today there's no more pirates therefore I can't be a pirate. I know I can't be a pirate. I know I can't be a pirate because there're no more pirate ships.

In 1574 there were pirate ships.

By that time the total halt of legal, or national, European wars forced the French and German soldiers either to disappear or to become illegal—pirates. Being free of both nationalistic and religious concerns and restrictions, privateering's only limitation was economic. Piracy was the most anarchic form of private enterprise.

Thus, at that time, in one sense, the modern economic world began. In anarchic times, when anyone could become any one and thing, corsairs, free enterprisers roamed everywhere more and more . . .

Murderers killed murderers . . .

Human beings are good by nature. This is the credo of those who are liberals, even pacifists, during times of national and nationalistic wars.

But in 1574, when regular, regulated war, that is, national war, which the nations involved had maintained at huge expense only via authoritarian expansion, ceased: the sailors the soldiers the poor people the disenfranchised the sexually different waged illegal wars on land and sea.

War, if not the begetter of all things, certainly the hope of all begetting and pleasures. For the rich and especially for the poor. War, you mirror of our sexuality.

I who would have and would be a pirate: I cannot. I who live in my mind which is my imagination as everything—wanderer adventurer fighter Commander-in-Chief of Allied Forces—I am nothing in these times.

DENNIS COOPER

George: Wednesday, Thursday, Friday

From the novel *Closer*

George streaked toward his room. "I'm home." He passed the kitchen door. His dad was drinking espresso. "George, wait . . ." He double-bolted his door. "I know it's here." He pawed through a desk drawer. At the bottom were two crinkled, typewritten pages.

They contained detailed descriptions, in French, of how he looked, smelled and tasted. Philippe had presented them to him a few weeks ago, with the words, "This is you in a—how you say—nutshell." "He should know," George thought. "Now if I buy a French dictionary . . ."

"George?" He dropped the pages and kicked them under his bed. "Just a second." He let his dad in. "Son, I thought we might go for a drive to the ridge and look down at the pretty lights. How about it?" That was the last thing George wanted to do. "I'm busy." "I just thought . . ." "*Really*, dad."

Mr. Mills wandered back to the kitchen. George lifted his Mickey Mouse cap, grabbed a tab of the acid he'd stashed there, and slipped it under his tongue. He set The Cramps' "Garbage Man" forty-five on his turntable. . . . *Do you understand? / Do you understand? . . .* By its end he was seeing things.

There was a huge map of Disneyland over his bed. He liked to stare at it, picture his favorite Lands or imagine new areas stocked with rides. Acid helped. He closed his eyes and, in ten seconds flat, he was tiptoeing through an attraction.

Room after room after room of incredible holograms. Over his head, a Milky Way of skulls snapping like turtles. He was knee-deep in a lime-green fog, scattered through which were see-through ghosts, skimpy as kleenexes. A booming, vaguely familiar voice wafted out of the camouflaged speakers. "Georges?"

"Shit, what time is it?" He opened his eyes. For a couple of seconds the ride and his bedroom were double-exposed like a photograph. The Goofy clock on his night table read six-thirty-seven. "I'm late," he gasped, shooting up to his feet. "Bye, dad." He slammed the front door.

He stood on the sidewalk and stuck out his thumb. A trucker chose him. The guy seemed friendly enough, but he kept asking personal questions. "Do you have a girlfriend?" he leered at one point. "Look, I'm on acid, so leave me alone, all right?" That shut him up. George hallucinated in peace.

He knocked. Philippe let him in. "Georges, uh, my friend Tom is here and I thought . . ." "Phil, he's a spectacle." It was an older man. He sort of looked like a stork wearing glasses. "Thanks," George said quickly. "Uh, Tom," Philippe said, "Georges and I will be very alone for a minute."

"I thought a change would be good," he continued, once Tom left the room. George was pissed off, but the acid made anger seem corny to him at that moment. More than anything, he was amazed by Philippe's eyes. They were unusually warm, but he felt even less warmth than ever from them.

"Be prepared and I will see you back here." George walked to the bathroom, stripped. He stared at the mirror while all sorts of scattered thoughts raced through his mind. None stayed long enough to complete themselves. "Later," he said aloud, popping a zit on his upper back.

He lay face down on the living room rug. Philippe's friend said some nice things about him. One of the two guys caressed his ass, then used some fingers to open its hole so wide George felt cold air rush in. "Maybe," Tom said, to which Philippe answered, "Good."

How had Philippe put it? "Your asshole looks like a child's pout . . ." George couldn't remember the rest. "Shit, baby." That was Philippe's voice, so George pushed a couple of turds out. "What does he normally eat?" Tom asked. "Hamburgers, french fries, candy bars . . ." "I could have guessed," Tom mumbled.

Two fingers slid up his ass. Since he'd met Philippe, George had learned how to count them. Two more joined in. He hadn't taken that many before. "Not bad," he thought. Someone felt for his lips, pried them open and four fingers slid down his throat. "He's got a big mouth," Tom whispered. "I love that."

George gagged a few times. "Let it loose," Philippe said in a soothing voice. George didn't want to, then he was vomiting. When that ran out he noticed most of Tom's hand was inside his hole. The other was fiddling around in his throat like it had dropped something.

Someone was spanking him. Picturing how his ass looked usually helped him relax. He knew the thing was bright red, but he couldn't imagine an arm sticking out of it. Maybe it looked like an elephant. If that was so, Tom's continual praise made more sense. "Really," George thought, "that *would* be great."

"Oh, God, I . . . take this child . . . beyond the . . . shit!" Some of the words were Tom's, some Philippe's. Come splattered over his ass, back and legs. Then the hands withdrew. "Is there anything else you want to understand?" That was Philippe's voice. "No, got it." Tom.

George sat up. He couldn't see very well, but he picked out Tom's glasses. "Do you have any idea how soft you are inside?" Tom asked. George felt incredibly stoned. He managed to say, "I guess." Philippe laughed. "You must have been fisted before." That was Tom again. "No." George shook his head.

Once George had showered and dressed, Tom gave him a lift.

All the way home Tom kept asking if he had enjoyed himself, then if he liked playing dead, then if he'd thought about killing himself. "I'm not sure. Maybe. Not really." "Just between us," he said, "if you decide to go all the way, call me. I'm in the book."

George lay in bed wondering what the guy meant by "all the way." Did that mean Tom would dissuade him, or did that imply he'd assist? George decided to jot down the guy's number, just in case. He tiptoed into the hall, scanned the phone book and crept back to safety.

He looked around at his room. There was the Disneyland map; there the poster of Pluto, his ears flying up in the air; there the Mickey and Minnie desk lamp; there the oval-shaped mirror with Donald Duck chasing his nephews around the frame. He struggled up, took the mirror from its nail.

He laid it out on the floor. He pulled his ass open, hoping to see what the men were so wild about. He could have guessed it'd resemble a cave, but, with the swelling and stuff, it looked exactly like Injun Joe's Cave, his eighth or ninth favorite Disneyland ride at the moment.

He'd stumbled on it five years ago. Even though, once inside, it was a slight disappointment—too narrow and crowded—he still made a beeline for it at least once every visit and spent a while outside its painted mouth, squinting into the dark, covered with goose bumps.

He climbed into bed and was almost asleep when he thought of his diary. He hadn't written in it for weeks. Once he'd thought it would empty him out. But those writings were no help. They just kept his feelings from getting lost. "Still, why not?"

"Drugs are finally getting to me. I'm going through things I guess I shouldn't because it seems fun, but it isn't. Does that make sense? I don't know anymore, and I don't really care. Life's sort of out of control, though I guess that's my own stupid fault.

"I think the last time I wrote Cliff and I were best friends. He changed a lot. We wave to each other at school, but that's it. I shouldn't have let him have sex with me. He told me we would be friends for eternity. He said a lot of things. All shit.

"This is so boring. I guess that's why I stopped writing. I'm fucked up. I don't know what to do. I don't even think I'm alive anymore. I'm walking around but I'm not really there. If I didn't have sex with Philippe I'd go nuts.

"School's nothing. I hate my friends. Nobody's interested in me anymore. They think I'm cute then they get really bored. If I don't sleep with people they hate me. But when I do they think they know me or something. I hope not.

"I don't know what I should call Philippe. He doesn't love me, I guess. It's weird he's not getting bored, but that's because he pretends I'm dead. I can't understand what that stuff's all about. But I don't mind. It doesn't matter.

"I've been trying to make myself great for a long time. I know I'm too closed around people, but when I talk, like with Cliff, it doesn't make any difference. I can still be amusing sometimes, except it's more like just weird lately.

"I keep saying I'll change and I want to. But all I do is get tense. That's okay for a while. Acid's great but I think stupid things while I'm on it. I still dream of living in Disneyland. I don't know how long I've been saying that.

"I guess I hope something fantastic is going to happen. I don't think it's up to me. I'll try but it's hard to say stuff like that without getting bored. Like right now I'm totally bored. I don't understand that."

George felt like shit. The clock focused. Seven-twelve. He dressed and ran to the bus stop. His shirt was on inside out. "Shit." He climbed in and sat behind Jerry Cox. George liked to look at the back of his head. His hair was blond, wavy, thick. It made George think of a crystal ball. He planned the day ahead.

At school he hit the head, took some acid. He was hallucinating all morning. Algebra, Woodshop and History drifted past, like puffy clouds when he laid on his back. At noon he dumped his textbooks in his locker and filled up a tray in the lunch room. Paul was waiting for him at their usual table.

After a few minutes Sally and Max, her new boyfriend, joined in. Max told some racist jokes. Sally constructed a tower of Pepsi cans and dubbed it "George Miles Nude." They shared an angry look. Paul pointed out a drug dealer who sold "the best grass in the universe." George made a mental note.

George was taking his last bite of spice cake when Fred, a dumb jock, wandered by. The guy always made fun of him, so George ignored the creep. "Hey, fag," Fred said as he sauntered by, "I hear you're lousy in bed." George pretended he hadn't quite heard that.

"George, what . . ." "Forget it, Paul." Sally piped in: "What's this about? Something wrong, George?" He tried to play it cool. "No, nothing. It's just some bullshit a former best friend of mine's spreading around." Sally's face whitened. "Gee, I thought *I* was your former best friend." "Jesus," George thought.

Ten minutes later George saw liar David sit down at the next table. He leaned over and yelled, "I hear you're Cliff's latest fuck." David blushed, spilled some milk down his shirt. "Oh, hi. I didn't think you would mind. I admire you a lot." George scowled and left him in peace. "Anyway, Sally . . ."

The bell rang. George waved goodbye. He was heading for Chemistry class when he thought he heard, "Hey, Miles." Mr. McGough pinned his head in a vice grip, dragging him into an empty classroom. "Got any grass, addict?" "No, fucking let me go!" "Oh, such a tough kid," the teacher laughed.

George drew up his courage. "When are we going to hang out?" "Ahem," McGough grinned, "I like you, George. You know that. If I were gay . . ." But George knew he was gay. He'd propositioned Paul recently, then thrown a fit when it didn't work out. Next thing Paul knew, there was a giant red F on his book report.

There was no point in confronting McGough. He'd never drop his guard. "See ya," George said. "Fuck it," is what he meant. He was a few minutes late for class, but no problem. He poured the blue liquid in with the yellow stuff and brought the goo to a boil. Blub, blub, blub.

$CO_2 + NO$ = nitrogen oxide or some such shit. He'd never made sense of any of it. He watched the second hand spinning around and around and around. On his way to the bus, he took the rest of his acid. The trip home was better than usual. They almost hit an old man in a crosswalk.

He slammed the front door and stopped in the kitchen. "I want your ass here, now, this second!" It was his dad's voice. George strolled to the den, threw himself on the couch. Puff, their Siamese cat, got confused and leapt off. "What's this?" his dad bellowed, holding some paper up. It was Philippe's list.

George thought, "If I tell him the truth I'll have to sneak out from now on. But if I say it's a joke he'll think I'm crazy and then what?" He had to say something. "Someone I slept with once gave that to me. I thought it was weird, but she wants to be a biology teacher."

"What's the girl's name?" "Forget it! I'm not going to tell you that. She's just a strange girl. Besides, it's been months. Let's drop it." "No, this is serious, George," his dad shouted, "I know a little French. I've never seen such filth!" Phlegm flew out of his mouth when he got to the *f*.

George saw his chance to escape. "How dare you spit on me!" He rose to his feet. His dad shoved him back on the couch. "I'm taking you to see someone," he said. "Maybe she can do something. I give up. Get your coat." George trotted into his room, swearing under his breath.

Drawers had been yanked out and dumped on the bed, posters ripped up, books thrown about. George was amazed by how flimsy his kingdom had been. One person brought the thing tumbling down. Then he remembered his diary. He shoved his arm under the mattress. It was there, locked tight. "Phew!"

George was surprised when their car stopped in front of a hospital. "I thought you meant a psychiatrist," he moaned. His dad shook his head. "Just go in. She's in room thirty-nine, on the top floor.

I'll be back in an hour." George entered the place thinking, "I'm not nearly stoned enough."

A nurse saw him traipsing around the halls. "You look like you're lost," she smiled. George admitted that he was. The address plate for room thirty-nine had apparently fallen off. She gave the door a push. "You're on your own." Inside, his mom was asleep. It looked permanent.

There was a video monitor near his head. A little light was drawing mountains across it. George watched for a while. It wasn't interesting. It was like one of those odd things that came on a tv screen after a station went off for the night. Was it trying to say something?

He listened to the mechanical whirr of the monitor. Once he thought he heard a scratchy voice say, "This is it." "Oh!" Some nurse, a new one, had walked in. "You must be this woman's son. Just a minute, I'll wake her up." Before George could say, "Don't," she'd rustled her way to the bed.

She squeezed his mom's shoulder. Her eyes flipped open. She glanced around. "Your child's here," the nurse chirped. She left. George and his mother looked blankly at each other. "Hi. Dad dropped me off." She didn't say anything, so George peeked at the monitor. It held the same boring image.

By the time he got back to her face she was opening and closing her mouth. Finally sounds came out. "George," she sighed, then, after several more jaw movements, "yes." This was what George had expected. She'd become scary. He wanted some acid.

She was trying to talk again. "Your father," she wheezed, "told me . . . something." Her face scrambled in an attempt to remember. George couldn't think how to distract her. He smiled, hoping she'd tell him how cute he was. Eventually she did, not in so many words, but her eyes said it. Or he assumed they had.

He glanced out the window. All he could see was the wall of another wing. One of its windows was open and, though the insides were dark, he heard a tv set. That's where that voice must have come from. He couldn't tell what was on, maybe news or a soap opera. Something too serious.

"Nice day," he said. His mom appeared to agree. "So, school's going fine. You know me, I try . . ." He talked about every uninteresting thing he could think of. She watched him. At least her eyes were pointed his way. They could have been saying, *You're cute*, or, *It's a nice day*, or, *Go on*."

He looked at the monitor. Its puny mountains were gone. There was a light jetting over the screen, a straight line being started again and again. It made him think of John, pencil to paper, erasing, redrawing, until he had gotten George right. When that thought disappeared, he saw the light.

He'd seen that happen in movies. He knew what it meant. He stared at his mom for a while. Then he stood up, walked into the hall and stopped the first nurse he saw. "Mom's . . . shit . . . dead." She yelled to another nurse, who came running. "Where?" they asked, kind of angrily. "The room with no number," George said.

He sat on a low brick wall near the hospital entrance. He watched people go in and out. As they approached the door it sensed their presence and swung open. There were doors like that everywhere, but he'd never thought about them before. He stood and inched toward it. When he was five feet away it opened.

The car drove up. George climbed in. They'd already gone a few blocks when his dad asked, "How is she?" George thought a second. "Dead." He was glad when his dad didn't say anything. They made a U-turn, parked, locked up and walked toward the entrance. When they were five feet away from the door it opened.

"Well, it's over. She's dead. I don't know what I'm supposed to think. I just wish I wasn't there when it happened. Dad thinks it's my fault. He didn't say so, but I can tell. Shit, he's the one who upset her. He did it, not me. I was just there.

"I'm going to use this to make myself change, like a starting point. I think that's the best thing to do. I won't buy any more drugs. I'll try not to do what I always do. I never do anything other than school and Philippe.

"Tomorrow I'll clean up my room and make it look like a normal place. I think I'll burn all my Disneyland stuff so I can't change my mind. Nobody else was ever interested in the stuff anyway and all my feelings for it are destroyed by the drugs now.

"I called Cliff tonight, just to talk. He doesn't care anymore. He kept saying how cute David was. I guess they're in love. He said that David is sort of obsessed or whatever with me. I don't know why, but it pisses him off. I hung up.

"It's strange I'm not sad about mom. I guess it took such a long time I felt everything I could feel already. I wish I hadn't been there, but I'm glad the last person she looked at was me. She really loved me once. Likewise, I guess.

"I think I'm afraid of stuff. Maybe that's it. I was afraid mom would die, but now she has and it's okay. I can't let it stop me from doing things. I'm going to keep that in mind from now on. I mean it.

"I'm not ready to sleep. I have one hit of acid left. I've decided to take it and go visit Tom, Philippe's friend. It's like a party or something to say my goodbye to the person I am. I'll let you know what happens. I'm off."

George sat on a couch, sipping gin from a tumbler. Tom was building a fire in the fireplace. George was sufficiently high, but the way Tom was watching the flames made him jumpy. "So, whatcha been up to?" Tom jabbed a log with an iron bar. George tried again. "Nice place." He meant the paintings.

"A friend did them." Tom set down the bar. "My friend believes corpses dream," he said. "Try to imagine each work is the dream of a murdered child." George couldn't. "Poor baby. School hasn't done you a lick of good, has it?" George could relate to that. "Nope."

"But you don't need to know anything, do you? Your beauty is far more profound than the works of our fine intellectuals, don't you think?" "I don't know," George chortled nervously. "What a bizarre thing to say." Tom wandered over and kissed, or rather, sucked George's mouth as if it were a snakebite.

George laughed so hard he spilled his drink on his shirt. Tom ripped it open. "Hey," George said, "I need to wear this tomorrow." "Don't kid me," Tom snapped. "You know you won't need a shirt." George didn't know what that meant, but he was too stoned to fight. "Okay, I'm sorry. Go on. Really."

George's new jeans got the same treatment. Next thing he knew everything he'd had on was turning black in the fireplace. Tom dragged him onto the rug, did the vacuuming bit on his ass. George tried to shit, but he just hadn't eaten enough. "That's okay," Tom said, and wiped his mouth. "I get the idea."

"Wait here." Tom left the room. George stretched his legs. He'd begun to hallucinate slightly. He kept confusing the windows and paintings. "It's about time," he thought. Tom was a creep but now things wouldn't matter so much. He was about to go over and refill his tumbler when Tom came back.

"Lie on your stomach," he barked. George did. He heard a clinking noise, and felt a tiny sharp pain in his ass. "It's just some novocaine," Tom muttered, "so I can take you apart, sans your pointless emotions." "That's considerate," George thought. Just then his ass grew so numb he felt sliced in half.

"Let's go." George, walking unsteadily, followed the man down a steep flight of stairs. Maybe it was the numbness but he couldn't see very well. There was something on one of the walls, a shelf? Things piled all over it? Tom took a piece of the blur in his hand. It looked fun. No, it looked kind of dangerous.

Tom raised the blur to the level of George's chest. "Do you know what's inside that cute body of yours?" George didn't have any idea, but he couldn't risk sounding naive. "I think I do." "Really?" Tom said. "You might be surprised. Would you like to know?" George shrugged. That seemed the safest response.

George was about to cry. He was right on the edge. He had to hand it to Tom. He couldn't remember the last time he'd been so upset. When Tom indicated the floor, George went flat. He heard a series of sounds. The only thing they remotely resembled was somebody chopping a tree down.

Tom didn't talk for a while. The sounds continued. George listened attentively. He realized he was being chopped down. He sort of wished he could know how it felt, but Tom was right. He'd be crying his eyes out and miss the good parts. It was enough to see his blood covering the floor like a magic rug.

The strange-sounding music stopped. George heard a soft voice. "Any last words?" it asked. George was surprised by the question. If he was supposed to be dead, how could he talk? Still, why not? "Dead . . . men . . . tell . . . no . . . tales," he said in his best spooky voice.

When Tom didn't laugh George bit his lip. That's all it took. He burst into tears. He felt a couple of slashes across his back. "I said no fucking emotions!" Tom yelled. "Do you want me to kill you or not?" "No," George sobbed. "Well, then what are you doing here?" "I don't know," George blubbered, "I don't know."

He was rolled onto his back. Through his tears he saw Tom's glasses. "Get out of here!" They came flying off. "Now! Stand!" George struggled up to his feet. "I don't have anything to wear," he choked. Tom stormed out of the room, then came back with a blanket and threw it at George's head.

George made his way to the door. "No, this way," Tom said, forcing open a small window near the ceiling. "You'll drip all over my house!" George dragged himself through the dusty rectangle. A hand grabbed his ankle. "Don't tell anyone how this happened," Tom hissed. "You're dead if you do."

George stumbled home, crumpling to the sidewalk occasionally. When headlights appeared in the distance he hid in the closest bush. The walk took hours. The blanket was no help at all. It got soaked with blood and grew very cold. He'd cry a while, then shiver, which made him cry again.

The house was dark. He climbed through his window. When he saw the ruins of his room it made him cry again. He found a note from his dad on the foot of the bed. *David called. Who's he?* "Good question," George thought, "and I've got a better one." He scrounged around in the rubble and found his mirror.

His ass wasn't really an ass anymore. He couldn't look at it. He dropped the mirror. It shattered. He walked down the hall and knocked twice on his dad's door. After a minute it opened. George looked in the man's puffy eyes. "Umm," he whispered, "I think you should call for an ambulance."

CATHERINE TEXIER

The Fedora

Jimmy tells me this story: he was on his way to fly to London, and when he got to West Fourth Street, to board the train to the plane, he realized he still had his switchblade in his jeans pocket. There was no way he could walk through the metal detector with a weapon in his pants. And what was the point of hiding it away in his suitcase (which can be searched anyway)? A blade is a blade and a hand must be able to pull it in a fraction of a second if the situation calls for it. Better not have it at all. Better leave it in New York where it belongs. He ran to the end of the station. As the train pulled along the platform he looked around for a hiding place. The ceramic tiles against the back wall were not flush with the ground. He quickly inserted the blade in the narrow groove running along the platform edge and jumped in the subway car between the closing doors. A month later, back from Europe, he went to look for the knife. It was still there, untouched, but somewhat rusted.

He pulls it out of his pocket, still rusted. He switches it open. It flashes in the light of the overhead lamp. He lovingly strokes it and checks the point with a finger. Then he kisses me.

———

On top of the orange dune, his body stretched under the sun. From below it seemed oversized, a huge head and torso, haloed with sunlight, towering over the ocean. She started to climb the sharp slope, digging deep sand funnels with her heels. She yanked her sandals off, held them up in salute, and walked on barefoot towards him, lifting her skirt. He stood there, motionless, almost black against the glaring light. When she arrived near him, he moved his hands up her legs and pressed them against her bare buttocks. The sand is burning me, she said, hopping on one foot, then the other. Together they ran to the cool waves below.

I have kept a picture of my mother. In the picture she is about forty-five, fifty. It is summertime and she is standing in the middle of a field, wearing a short-sleeved printed dress. There is a white fence behind her, bordering on a cluster of dark trees, which for some reason I always took to be the edge of a cemetery, and she appears to be staggering, overwhelmed with tears and sadness, even though it seems more likely that she was just blinded by the light, her eyes squinting in the sun.

Why do I think she is coming out of a cemetery? When I was growing up she hated funerals and talking about death. She avoided the issue altogether. Maybe she thought if she ignored it enough, death would pass her by.

But really, all I am worried about is that the man with the dark felt hat and the black overcoat—he cuts an unexpected Maigret silhouette on Lower Broadway—will follow me again on my way home. I have never seen his eyes. All I know of him is his back, the big tailored shoulders surmounted by a fedora, and the dry squeaking of his leather shoes on the sidewalk behind me. I don't turn around when I hear them. I duck my neck and head for my doorway. I catch a glimpse of him only after my key is already inserted in the lock and halfway turned. He walks rather slowly, his shoulders a little bent.

— — —

My neighbor comes down for tea and cookies on Saturday afternoon. She likes her tea very sweet and without milk. Sometimes
she brews it with mint, Moroccan style. Her hands with fingernails
cut short are small and she is extremely good with them. They
flutter around like butterflies when she talks. We make at least
two pots of tea. We sit around the kitchen table near the back
window where the morning glories grow in late summer and in
winter when it gets dark one of us pulls the cord of the overhead
lamp. She tells me stories of walled-in Arab towns and tales of
strong-smelling Mediterranean shores. She wears her thick hair
down to her waist in a long sweep of shiny black, sometimes brushes
it to the side, weaving it in a single braid hanging over one shoulder. She works for Pan Am at a ticket counter and is entitled to
special rates on international flights, which enables her to go to
Cairo twice a year to visit her family. She likes thin blond men,
cool and streetwise with a mean streak, who always end up fucking
her up. We swap advice about men that we both follow to the
letter. Neither of us seem to have much success in finding, let
alone keeping, a good one. Jimmy excepted, that is. From time to
time she hennas my hair. I sit on the toilet lid, my shoulders
wrapped up in a towel, while she kneads the brown powder to a
thick paste that she applies on my skull in parallel furrows. She
works with her bare hands. She says she gets a better feel of what
she is doing with no gloves on. She comes out of these sessions
with palms the same orange-brown as my hair which takes days
to wash off, but she doesn't mind. She says in her country women
draw delicate designs with henna on the palms of their hands and
the soles of their feet, kind of like soft tattoos, that are extremely
praised.

I never told Leila (it's my neighbor's name) about the man with
the fedora. I never told anybody. Sometimes I don't see him for
days and I believe I made him up, or perhaps he is a childhood
memory that I reincarnate in different men.

— — —

Jimmy is a musician. He plays rock 'n' roll in local clubs late at night. I met him in the street, he had just played a gig with his band. They were putting their instruments down and getting ready to collect money when I walked by. They all made comments on me, the kind of jokes men tell at the sight of a pretty girl, except these were nice, and funny.

Yo, mami, look at that hat. Why're you hiding your eyes like that? Nice mouth, though.

I had bright red lipstick on.

Hey, don't go away. We'll play something special for you, okay?

I leaned against a lamppost and they played a soft tune with a nice melody. They were pretty tough and grubby-looking, hair dyed blue-black and leather jackets loaded down with metal studs, except the lead guitar who was tall and skinny with delicate, long racy hands, his hair sleeked back and a narrow kind of intellectual face with sensual lips. There was like a little wicked flame in his eyes each time he smiled and I liked that. He held my hand a bit longer than he had to when I left, and the sweetness of his touch stayed with me.

The shack was standing right on the Atlantic Ocean in southern Morocco, at the edge of a small piece of land that belonged to a farmer's family. Just behind it were growing rows of tomato plants and a few orange trees bearing overly sour fruit. They spent their evenings at the farmhouse, sitting cross-legged near the *brasero*, dipping chunks of flat warm bread in the cumin-spiced juices of the *tajine*, then silently watched the farmer, an old man with parched hands, prepare his kif, chopping up marijuana and tobacco leaves on a small bench squeezed between his thighs, mincing them down to a fine powder they smoked with him in a narrow wooden pipe.

Being with you is everything I ever wanted, he said, stoned, his eyes unfocused. Later, in the shack, he went down on her, pushing her skirt up her hips, and sucked the juice out of her as she moaned, do it, oh do it, I love you, and flipped herself on her stomach, ass so tempting.

My typewriter sits on a metal typewriter table painted by its previous owner in a sunny yellow enamel, chipped here and there. It's a Smith-Corona with a correcting device. In the three side drawers I keep a ream of white bond paper, several bottles of white-out (brand Liquid Paper) that I use when I have to erase a whole line or make corrections on the carbon copy, a purple snail-shaped container of Taperaser, two black and white nylon ribbons, a bottle of correcting fluid for when the white-out thickens, also from Liquid Paper, a small stapler, a box full of paper clips and a few erasers. My pencils and felt-tip pens are gathered in a beige mug with chocolate-brown stripes, next to the picture of my mother clipped in a clear plastic frame. I have a gray nylon cover to keep the dust off the typewriter when not in use. Most of the time I work in an office uptown, every day, that is, from noon to six, but I also take on freelance typing, M.A. or Ph.D. theses, plays, screenplays, whatever.

A man on a horse gallops by, raising clouds of smoke at his flanks. He is in hot pursuit of some villains, themselves breathlessly galloping through an arid and moonlike section of a southwestern desert. Suddenly a shrill whistle cuts through the clop of horseshoes and the man stops dead in his tracks. His face is deeply furrowed and sunburnt. He pushes his hat back and wipes his forehead with an air of puzzlement. And then everything blurs because Jimmy has pulled up my sweater and his hand touches one of my breasts and his lips my lips and I can sniff his breath with a taste of Scotch and grass mixed in and there is a male smell coming from all over him, sweat and tobacco and warm skin and the layers of his flannel shirt and T-shirt, the edge of his collar against my lips, the taste of his neck in my mouth, my hand on his shoulder, under his clothes, searching for naked skin, anywhere, a place to touch, a place to hold on to.

— — —

The farmer left when the moon rose. His friends had come to pick him up, white teeth flaring in the half-open door, an air of conspirators under their woolen hats dark as night. He followed them barefoot, his *cirouel* floating around his scrawny legs, they vanished toward the shore without a sound. The farmer knew the stars, the Great and the Little Dipper, the Milky Way, the Northern Star, the position of the planets. They became paler as the moon went up, yellow pumpkin turning into silver disk. He stood on the dune, waiting for it to rise high in the firmament, then sat down, filled up his *sebsi* with kif and smoked until his eyes were about to close. Then he walked down to the foot of the dune, and lay down, dog-like, wrapped in his brown *djellaba*.

When I split up with my former boyfriend I left behind in his apartment a photo that I liked very much. It was a close-up of me taken by a photographer I used to know. She was a good enough artist to catch you off guard, and capture something you would normally let go only in an intimate moment. Something raw, almost indecent. When you looked at the picture you felt you got a glimpse of it almost by accident. Then you had to take another look to make sure. And you might not find it again. The print was tacked on the wall over the dresser, and it didn't occur to me to take it, it seemed to belong there. Perhaps it was a way of leaving a little bit of me behind, in compensation for running away. But lately I have been thinking about that picture. It's been like an ache. I have been wanting to hold it very badly. To keep it as a witness, of past times maybe. To hang it on my own wall, over my own dresser. To own it. So I wrote to him. He doesn't live in this city anymore. It took him a long time to reply. And, what with the job and the things to do, I had almost forgotten about it. But then I got a letter from him saying that he felt the picture was his now because I never reclaimed it, and he was sentimentally attached to it, as a memory of our affair. I told Leila I thought it was a load of crap because we hadn't been together that long, and anyway I had heard he was living with somebody. In a way, though, I was flattered, but his response upset me. I answered him back angrily.

And here we are all of a sudden bickering back and forth by letter, and then by phone over an 8 by 10 photo, maybe already yellowed by exposure to the light, as if it were a vintage print.

In winter it is pitch black when I get off the subway after work. I go down Broadway a little ways, then I make a left on Great Jones, and I keep walking, way east. After the Bowery, when Great Jones becomes East 3rd, the flow of people thins out—the bums don't stagger very far from the men's shelters—and I try to stay on the edge of the sidewalk or, if there is no traffic, right in the light of the street lamps that throw big orange halos on the pavement. I am not scared of muggers, I know how to handle myself on the street, but when I hear his shoes creaking, my heart misses a beat. He's taken me by surprise this time. Usually he starts following me right after Broadway. We are alone on the street. The wind howls at the intersections. I push my hat way down on my face, I keep my hands deep in the pockets of my overcoat. There is no car coming, no sound other than the clatter of soda-pop cans and the rustling of newspaper pages pushed by the wind. His shoes hit the sidewalk in an even, unhurried way. I keep my heartbeat in check. I don't walk any faster. Why give him the alarm. We fall into the same rhythm, him maybe fifteen steps behind me. I can see us: two black figures with hats, fastened together in an urban walk on a desolate street of Manhattan, throwing eerie shadows onto abandoned cars crouching in the gutter like dead horses along the prairie highways.

I am lying on my bed, knees folded, in socks, long johns and T-shirt. The steam hisses in the valve, high on the riser, then claps it shut. I've got a tall glass of gin and tonic on the night table, a stack of magazines on one side of me, *Mademoiselle* and *Glamour* and *Vogue*, and a plate of cheese and crackers on the other. My nibbling has made a serious dent in the half-pound of Cheddar but I have no intention of getting up and cooking a real dinner. The TV is on, the sound low, with a Katharine Hepburn/Spencer Tracy movie that I haven't been able to identify so far. I listen to the noises from the street but everything is quiet, and I've made sure my door locks are bolted. I will the phone to ring, real bad, but it's dead by my drink. The silence spreads, folds and folds of it, fluid as time.

They made love by candlelight on the mud floor of the shack, the wooden shades open to the sea, each of their moves mirrored by long shadows flickering up and down the wall. After coming she watched his face dissolve into pleasure, bathed in the moonrays of an African night, that every morning, without fail, exploded into a dazzling sun.

Jimmy walks into my apartment and throws his scarf on the back of a chair. His leather jacket smells good against my nose. He goes to the fridge, pops open a Budweiser and collapses on the couch. He doesn't say a word. I know something is fishy the way he balances the can between his legs.

So how are things?

Alright I guess.

He is looking at the floor, past his beer.

Listen, he says. I can't go out with you tonight.

Why?

We've got to rehearse. I didn't know about it. I mean it was just confirmed this afternoon. There's a studio that's going to be free for a few hours.

I think he is lying, but I am not sure. He might just be feeling guilty at letting me down. After all he could've just called me up. Why bother coming all the way?

B'slama, said the fisherman from the door. As they hastily got dressed, he squatted before the *brasero* set up in front of the shack, and started the fire, fanning it with a piece of cardboard. He had brought an armful of fresh mint and the flat bread that opens up in two moist lips when you cut it in half. He looked preoccupied, drawn. There had been an accident on the beach, during the night, when the tide was rising. A tourist's body thrown against the cliff.

Slashed. Gutted. It turned out it was a young English punk they had put up for a few nights while he was waiting for money to be wired from home. They were summoned to the morgue to identify his body, being the only people on the beach who knew his name or anything about him.

After the accident they grew restless, the very quality of the air seemed to change, to thicken.

I have this thing about edges. I can't stand them frayed or uneven. Take paintings, for instance. They've got to be perfectly parallel to the edge of a wall, or I'll scream. Stamps have to be cleanly ripped along the dented edges, and I would never glue one with the outside border of the stamp sheet still affixed to it. I can't help thinking that a person who arranges her stamps haphazardly on an envelope, upside down or dancing the jig somewhere in the vicinity of the upper right corner, ought to be suspected of low intellect, or such acute sloppiness it borders on mental disorder. A hem that's not straight can throw me off for hours. I always cut the butter at square angles with the length of the stick and make sure it doesn't get full of jelly or smear the edges of the butter dish.

Jimmy doesn't get this. He thinks *I'm* the one who's mental. When he sleeps at my place he tosses his dirty socks and underwear about the bedroom so that they land on the radiator or the night table. He thinks it's going to make me angry, as if I was a nagging housewife or something. But he's way off base. I don't care about order or sloppiness in my home. It's just a question of straight angles.

Sometimes I lie down in front of the TV and I think of becoming very rich. I look at magazines and I dream of this kitchen, big, flooded with sun, set up like an exquisitely refined dining room, with powder-blue plates and cups, and a blue-gray pitcher standing on a blond pine dresser next to a brass jug ready to water the plants lushly gathered on the windowsills. I stare at pages and pages of evening gowns caked with beads, at racy satin or snake pumps on arched fuck-me heels, at smoked stockings running two dizzying straight seams from the ankles up, at Cartier watches of smooth extra-flat gold with the hours in roman numerals. I can't get my eyes off the stately entrance porch of this Georgian mansion, off that English garden crowded with rose bushes tumbling down the arbor. I am not a girl who likes diamond rings or gold hearts hanging from a chain, I wish for a Mark IV with silver paint.

Leila and I consult the I Ching to know if Jimmy is coming or going. Not that I think he is Mr. Right. But we'd like to know what he is up to. If you want, I could check the tea leaves after that, she offers.

In the middle of a vacant lot, used as a junkyard for trashed-out refrigerators, children's carriages, bedsprings and mattresses, sits a skinny black kid, perched on a stack of wooden crates. He's got a leather cap on, and one of his legs is crossed over the other. In his hands shines a trumpet that he brings up to his mouth. He plays jazz, a clear, bittersweet, humorous blues that cascades down the string of empty lots, echoing through the gutted buildings behind him. It is a cold winter day and all he is wearing is a pair of ripped jeans and an oversized dungaree jacket snapped up to his neck. His hands are bare.

It is 1:30 A.M., I am on my way home from a late late movie when I hear his steps behind me. He is off schedule. He's never followed me this late. I clench my teeth and bravely walk on. He is so close behind me I can see the shadow of his fedora jump ahead of us when we pass the street lights. We go from block to block. I know this time is *it*. He is going to make his move, press his sleeve around my chest and push his thumb in the middle of my neck until I stop breathing. Or he'll open his big overcoat and zip down his pants. He'll pull out his dick, it'll be big and somewhat flabby and he'll push it against my thighs. Or he'll drag me to the vacant lot across the street . . . He is so close now, one more step and . . . He is next to me . . . He passes me . . . He walks on, his leather soles playing their little music on the pavement, his big shoulders, his thick nape neatly folded over his collar, his fedora with the narrow brim sitting on his skull, its two humps like a camel's back.

A big loft at the eastern edge of Soho in a part of the neighborhood that hasn't yet been given over to yuppies, United Nations consultants, advertising art directors or TV producers. Three walls of windows, floor to ceiling. Industrial gray carpeting, a few partitions in the middle, going halfway up. Five Lisas, one Macintosh and two IBM PCs are scattered on black tables throughout the wide space, most of them on, with green messages or stylized drawings flickering across the screens. A little office is set up at one end of the loft, decorated with odd furniture in Day-Glo colors.

A peroxide-blond male secretary, wearing khaki pants, an immaculate white shirt, black Weejuns and no socks, is sitting at a desk, a gold-tip pen fluttering between two fingers. A young woman, whose hair is closely shaven above her right ear, is helping herself from an electric drip-type coffee maker, then walks to the office, and hands the heat-resistant polyurethane cup to the secretary. Six stories below, the traffic is bustling on Broadway.

I ring the sixth floor in the commercial elevator. The metal door opens directly into the loft. A red-haired girl comes to greet me, immediately followed by a thin blond man, one hand extended, the other one holding a cup of coffee. Nice meeting you. He motions vaguely behind him. Coffee? As I decline he precedes me into his office. It's very warm. The window ledge made of some kind of metallic material glitters in the sun. I drop my coat on it, and wait. The secretary shows me around, asks me if I know how to use the word processors. I tell him I've fooled around with a friend's machine, but it was a Kaypro. He says it's okay. The software they have is very simple to use, and they'll let me try my hand at it before I start the job anyway. You'll have to sleep here until the work is completed, he says, taking me to a half-moon-shaped partition, lacquered peach-cream, behind which a futon is unfolded, with a comforter thrown on it. What do you mean, sleep here? I ask him. Of course we'll set you up comfortably, he goes on, paying no heed to my question, and pulls a chair balanced on three feet into the bedroom area, presumably to make it look more cosy.

How about your new job, asks Jimmy. I don't know, I answer, I feel like a prisoner in that place. For three days they didn't let me out. They said it was an emergency. They tripled my pay and made me work until 11, woke me up at 8 with a breakfast tray, ordered food, coffee, whatever I wanted, insisted on my taking breaks once in a while, a walk around the block with the red-haired girl; they even rented a movie for me to play on the VCR, *Last Tango in Paris*. I thought it was a little weird, their choice of film, I mean.

Jimmy smokes in silence, his eyes lost somewhere behind me. Pretty weird he says at last. You're sure they aren't going to kidnap you for white slavery or something? Who knows, I say. I don't know what they're up to. I don't like it, but how can I pass up the money?

The big window in front of me is clouded with frost, diffracting the light from the street. Lying wide awake on the futon, I listen to the muffled sound of voices coming from the other end of the loft. There has been a small dinner party, to which I haven't been invited. I was brought a plate of sashimi at my desk, while I finished typing a long section of a manuscript, my eyes getting increasingly tired before the blinking green cursor, my back stiffening against the swivel chair.

I saw the guests arrive, two men and a woman in evening clothes. My boss, whom I've been introduced to on the run once, as he was walking past my desk, and never saw again, greeted them at the elevator door. Dressed in a white silk shirt and tuxedo pants, he was busy pushing back a strand of hair that kept falling over his eyes. One of the men tossed his black silk cape in the arms of the red-haired girl in a manner that I found both princely and obnoxious. The woman wore her strapless gown and long black gloves with studied haughtiness. They moved down to the other end of the loft, behind the kitchen area, and quickly disappeared from my view. Later a caterer brought piles of spicy-smelling dishes that left a trail of cinnamon and cumin in the air.

One of them has a foreign accent, maybe French or Eastern European. I believe he is the one with the cape, the one at this instant pouring wine in the glasses that I hear clinking, or carefully setting his cup of coffee on its saucer and wiping his mouth, under the thin moustache, with a fine linen napkin.

Please get up, whispers a voice near me. Somebody is squatting a couple of feet away from my bed. The woman! I can make out her naked shoulders gleaming softly in the dark.

Hey! What . . .

Hushhh!

I smell her musky perfume, almost taste her lipstick as she bends toward me, whispers in my ear, her mouth brushing against my hair.

Please get up and get dressed, she repeats. I can't explain.

But as I am fumbling for my pants, that must be lying somewhere on the floor, she hands me some clothes and pushes them into my lap.

No. Put these on.

There's a long black dress of a satinlike material, garters and stockings and a pair of high-heel shoes, that she makes me slip on in the dark, hurriedly.

Morocco was hot, and dry. Arab boys sat thigh against thigh on low benches in windowless rooms, passing around the hashish pipe, listening to cassettes they kept in plastic shopping bags and played on cheap tape recorders, on and on the same repetitive tunes, getting high, their teeth flashing in their dark beautiful faces, holding hands, or arms wrapped around backs, heads so close together, swapping jokes in guttural Arabic rhythms. They drank sweet mint tea in small glasses that burnt the fingertips. The music swelled to a throbbing shrill. They banged with their closed fists on containers grabbed from around the room, a glass jar full of fresh mint for the tea, the tin sugar canister, makeshift drums marking the beat. One of them got up, arms extended, swirled around, gracious as a girl, his thin muscular body twisting with a sexy motion of the hips like a bellydancer from Khartoum.

She fastens a small velvet mask over my eyes, the kind used for Carnival, with two slits allowing you to see through, and leads me across the loft. They've left the dining table. Half-filled glasses, bottles and unfolded napkins are scattered on a lace cloth. The three men are comfortably arranged on a couch and armchairs, smoking cigarettes, coffee cups and round glasses of brandy at their elbows.

This is Justine, says the woman, introducing me around. Of course this is not my name, but I let it go. I figure, it goes with the mask. I bow to them, offer them a hand on which she has slipped a long suede glove studded with tiny red stones. They look at me with curiosity, one of them has piercing blue eyes and a languid mouth.

They offer me a glass of champagne and chat among themselves, ignoring me. Somebody puts a tape on. It's a slow sugary song from the fifties that prompts the woman to invite me to dance. She is taller than me, and again I smell her perfume around her neck. Her arm feels light on my waist, so much lighter than a man's, unsettling me. And when her hand moves up my bare back I prefer not to identify the waves it sends down my spine.

Her lips run up my thigh, teasing. I am half lying on a couch and she is kneeling before me. The men are pursuing an involved conversation in low tones, pulling on small fragrant cigars, seemingly oblivious of us. They get up and gather around a photograph or a small painting, I can't tell, and bend over it with what looks like a magnifying glass. Her gloved hands spread my legs open in a gentle but firm hold. Her tongue moves higher and higher, arouses my skin with small precise confident circles. Now she is sitting next to me, her naked breasts provocative in her low-cut dress, and we both have our skirts pulled way up, hands plunging deep in the flesh, thighs twisting; her cunt is soft and moist like cream under my fingers, tastes ripe in my mouth, and she groans, pushing my head against her. She stretches over me on the couch, half-naked, her eyes and makeup black as charcoal, and our bodies dance together, tight, grabbing ass, eating hair, mouth, mixing juices and sweat until we let go with long deep sighs.

Then I hear this voice behind us, cool, appreciative. Congratulations, Justine, it says, that was superb.

Jimmy is standing a few feet away from me, playing with his knife, testing its sharpness with the palm of his hand. He paces back and forth, his tension rising every time he turns around. I'll get them, he says. I'll get the fuckers. All his sound equipment has been stolen from the studio and his long black-clad figure twists with anger. He kicks a pile of books and sends them flying, some of them hit the wall and topple, land edge down, covers spread open like arms asking for mercy.

Jimmy, please . . .

Oh, shut up, alright?

He looks mean, his lips somewhat pulled up over his teeth, nostrils flaring. I'll get them, he snarls, switching his blade in and out.

He leaves, banging the door. He hasn't made love to me once since I came back from the loft. Leila sees a black-eyed woman in my cards, a queen of spades playing up to my fair-skinned knave.

They fought on the beach at dawn. It was low tide. The rocks laid bare by the withdrawing sea looked like a volcanic floor, all sharp needles and treacherous holes among which the agile-footed fishermen briskly hopped like fakirs. Their iron buckets quickly overflowed with mussels plucked from the rugged walls of small hollows still filled with seawater.

You're full of shit! You went to the shack and made out, right? How could you go off and fuck her, practically under my eyes?

They walked along the shore as the sun burst above the dune. She looked at him and her legs started to shake.

Bastard! Low-down motherfucker!

Will you please stop yelling.

Later he said, so what if I fucked her, as you say, so what?

She could tell just from the way the other girl was looking at him, a big German Valkyrie with pale hair and ocean-colored eyes that screamed I just got laid. She ran to the shack and huddled up on the mat. Sniffing about the covers for their smell she masturbated and came fifteen times in a row, picturing them in every lovemaking position she could possibly think up. Then she tiptoed out in the night, and sat wide-eyed on top of the dune, watching the tide lick its way down the beach.

Bastard! How could you do this to me.

He shrugged. She wasn't even a good fuck, he said. Had a pussy as big as a barn.

It's Saturday night. I eat Häagen-Dazs chocolate ice cream with chocolate chips. Then I send for Chinese food. I call Leila and invite her to come and share it with me. We watch a movie on TV while she bakes a middle-eastern pastry dripping with honey.

I thought Jimmy was the one, I tell her. He really makes me tick.

Give him time, she says. Men like that don't like to be pressured. They need free rein.

Don't you think I should call him, though? I've played it cool long enough.

She offers to wax my legs. She tells me I better take care of myself, have my hair cut. Another man might come along sooner than I think. You've got to get your power back fast, she says. Your self-confidence. As she spreads the burning wax with a wooden spatula in long swift motions of her wrist, I see the charcoal-black eyes of the woman in the loft glowing over mine.

I don't turn on Great Jones, I walk down Broadway, past Houston, elbow my way through the crowds pouring out of the subway station and the street peddlers pushing their wares along the sidewalk on small portable tables wobbly on the hardened snow. I walk a few more blocks and step into the gray building. I push the glass door and ring the sixth floor in the elevator. The door opens on a dark empty loft. Gone are the half-moon partitions, the computers, the funny furniture. It's just a huge rectangle lit up by the street lamps, full of shadows and a few cardboard boxes gaping in the middle.

I walk in, cross over to the wall of windows overlooking Broadway and sit on the metal ledge. The elevator door closes softly. All I can hear is the dampened sound of traffic from the street.

In the park the kids are screaming, pursuing each other with shrill cries, zigzagging between the strollers and the bicycles; a few winos warm their asses around a fire leaping neon-orange from a garbage can. I sit on a seesaw after having brushed the snow away. A bunch of skinheads are perched on the other ones, swinging up and down, up and down. One of the girls has a white cross edged with reddish purple painted on her cheek. I sit close to the middle of the seesaw and I swing gently, pushing with the tip of my toes.

Then I see Jimmy walk over to me, a woolen headband protecting his ears from the cold.

Hey, he says, touching my shoulders lightly with his hand. He goes around to sit at the other end of the seesaw. We swing a little for a few moments without saying a word. Once or twice I glance at him quick, but he keeps staring at the frosted twigs under his feet.

What are you doing here, he finally asks.

I shrug. I'm not sure I want to speak to him. Not yet. I think he owes me.

You wanna go for coffee?

I shrug again, ease down the wooden board. He jumps over it, passes an arm around me. I move my shoulders this way and that to tell him to lay off me. He shoves his hands in his pockets and starts whistling, taking big bouncing steps that force me to trot at his side. We walk like this through the park, slowing down in the street to keep from slipping on the thick and uneven coat of ice crusting the sidewalk, to the coffee shop at the corner. He sits across the table from me, blowing on his hands to warm them up. There's a hole in his sweater sleeve that, inexplicably, moves me. He is a tall, skinny kid who doesn't know what's what and especially how to take care of himself.

What happened at the loft? he asks.

Why?

I don't know. You haven't been the same since you came back.

How would you know? You haven't come near me.

I've been busy.

So?

Nothing.

Why have you been avoiding me? Are you seeing somebody else?

What? You're out of your mind. I told you I've been busy.

Oh yeah?

He sneers. Yeah.

It's a dead end. He's got that thin body, hair thick like freshly clipped fur. He smells the smell I like, his hips swing down the streets of Manhattan, his feet in run-down discolored Keds. He's got a mouth that melts my flesh away. He's got spring in his walk, a flame in his eyes, and a mean switchblade that he likes to impress girls with. He plays gigs at street corners, and in winter when it's too cold he sips hot mugs of weak coffee and sniffs lines of coke he scoops up with the tip of his blade. And I don't know if I give a fuck about him or not.

I've got this fur coat my mother left me. Or rather I took it from the place her furniture and all her things were kept in storage after they sent her body back to Baltimore. I saw the big black-green trunk that crowded her hallway and I opened it. They told me to pick the things I wanted. I hated her furniture. All this oak finish and fake brass buttons, the Chinese carpets made in Hong Kong, her army of doilies and vases bought at crafts fairs, needle-point knickknacks (she called them tapestries) she hung everywhere on her walls, now stacked on the floor in their dark brown frames. I wanted the leather chair my father used to sit on, its arms all chewed up by the cat's claws. But I didn't even have a place to put it. I'd just moved to a tiny apartment with two other kids, NYU students. So I opened the trunk and groped around, my arms deep in the layers of clothes, waves of mothball smell rising up to me. I felt the fur under my fingers and I pulled. It was her mouton coat she always wore in winter when I was growing up, with a round collar and sloping shoulders, I hadn't seen it in years. I stayed next to it for a while, balanced on the edge of the trunk, staring into some kind of void. Someone came to see what I was doing, what was taking me so long. I gathered the fur in my arms and signed a release paper in the office. Now I'm sitting on the rocking chair by the window, muffled up in the coat. It still smells of mothballs. I rock myself back and forth, back and forth, the big collar pushed up to my ears, held up with both my hands. The smell makes me sneeze. I try to think of her. All I remember is the greasy bacon she used to cook for us on Sunday morning, the only time when Dad was around, because he always worked night shifts, my little brother usually kicking me under the table. It's snowing out and I try to remember what was the last significant thing she said to me, something that would maybe express her feelings towards me or her philosophy of life or something, and all I can come up with is, you should always have a stock of tuna fish and ravioli in the pantry; it can come in handy. And I try and I try and I can't recall anything else. I'm stuck with the tuna fish when I'm looking for a legacy from my mother and the snow is starting to fall and the boiler must've broken down I guess because in the pale night the cold expands, a light frost covers the windowpane as dusk comes down and the faint sound of a trumpet rises from the vacant lot.

Tonight I will look at the window and from the shapes of steps in the snow I will try to guess who has been walking on the sidewalk.

— — —

Then I see him. His collar is turned up, his hat pushed down, his shoulders seem even more hunched than usual, his whole body contracted by the bitter wind. His face is drowned in shadow, but his figure is clearly delineated against the pearl glimmer of the snow, the fedora smartly creased in the middle, its outline sharper and sharper as he walks toward my house. I quickly move away from the window and wait. I think, he wouldn't dare. But he does. Like a single syncopated note dropped against the beat my buzzer rings. Once. Twice. A long interval, then a third time. And I sit, frozen, listening to the shrill, persistent pitch of the doorbell in the cold, abstract silence.

PETER CHERCHES
Dirty Windows

1. They met at a bookstore. She was thumbing through *Finnegans Wake* when he came by and said, "Nice weather." She liked that, so when he asked her to join him for a cup of coffee she agreed. They started talking and he learned that she was a meteorologist.

2. Early on in their relationship they agreed to proceed cautiously, so they hired extras to do the stunts.

3. They went to a motel for couples only. The sign in front promised erotic videos in each and every room, but when they tried the TV all they were able to get was a medical documentary titled "Strep Throat."

"I didn't come here for culture," he said, annoyed.

"What do you think we should do?" she asked.

"Well, we already paid our money," he said, "so let's go to sleep."

4. He went to take a look out the window. "Boy, your windows sure are dirty," he told her.

"My windows are clean," she said defensively. "It's your mind that's dirty."

5. He was watching her sing "The Star-Spangled Banner," one of the later stanzas, the one that begins "Oh thus be it ever." She was having trouble with the high notes. Then the doorbell rang. He ran to answer it, forgetting to put his pants on. It was a couple of Jehovah's Witnesses, a man and a woman.

"Armageddon will be a happy time," the woman said, ignoring his erection.

6. "I called you," she said, "but I got a message. It was in your voice and it said, 'You have reached a nonworking number.' I didn't know what to do, so I hung up."

"Was there a beep?" he asked.

"A beep?"

"Yes, a beep. After the message."

"I think so."

"You should have left a message," he said.

7. He was dreaming that she was telling him that if he didn't stop dreaming about her she would wake him up when he woke her up.

8. They were singing "One Hundred Bottles of Beer on the Wall" when halfway through they forgot the lyrics.

9. She was giving him a haircut when he started whistling. It was a strange tune, unlike anything she had ever heard before. She asked him about it and he explained that he was an anthropologist and that he had spent many years in a far-off land studying a most remarkable people who whistled these strange and beautiful songs while they made love. She was so engrossed in his story that she cut off all his hair.

10. He was imagining he was making love to another woman when he opened his eyes only to discover that she was another woman imagining she was making love to him.

11. "Your windows are dirty," she said to him.

"It's not my windows," he replied. "It's the world outside."

12. "Why are you doing this to me?" he asked her.

"Because I want to hurt you," she said.

"There are better ways to hurt me," he told her and he showed her what they were.

13. They went to a Halloween party as each other. The costumes were so good that nobody knew who they were.

14. It was a very large room and they had trouble hearing each other. So when he said, "I have a few things to do. I'll be going out for a while. I should be back in about an hour," she thought he said, "I lost my job and I owe everything we've got to a very big man. I've met another woman and I'm leaving you. Don't try to stop me."

15. They each placed an ad in the personals for a third party to join them. They were disappointed when they showed up to answer each other's ad.

16. She was taking a correspondence course in microsurgery. For assignment number three she had to cut him up into little pieces and put him back together. When she told him he said, "Forget it."

"I realize you're still upset about assignment two," she said, "but I assure you I'll do better this time."

He didn't say a thing. He just put his feet in his pockets and shook his head.

17. They had made a self-immolation pact, but he got cold feet and chickened out.

18. He couldn't get used to the new color she had painted the walls. It was a different kind of off-white, similar to the previous shade, but somehow disconcertingly different. He couldn't explain what it was that bothered him, but it bothered him. In fact, it made his skin crawl.

"Why couldn't you use the same color?" he asked her.

"They didn't have any more," she said.

"You should have gone to another store."

"It wouldn't have done any good," she said. "The man told me that the old color was discontinued. That this one was the closest thing."

After a moment of silence he said, "The closest thing—that's it!"

19. She read in a newspaper that he had been taken hostage in the Middle East. She was very angry, so she confronted him. "You don't tell me anything," she said, shoving the paper in his face. "I have to read it in the news."

20. "What's this?" he asked her, showing her the letter he had discovered.

"It's a love letter from another man," she told him.

"Then why is it in my handwriting?" he asked angrily.

"We did that to trick you," she told the other man.

21. They always used to take showers together until one day, they couldn't agree on the temperature.

22. He couldn't find the thing he was looking for. He looked everywhere. He was getting frustrated. Where was she? She'd know. He kept looking. He went through all the drawers. He even tried using a magnifying glass. No luck. Where the hell was she? He sat in the armchair and waited. When she returned several years later he said, "Where the hell were you?" She didn't say a word. She handed him a small package. It was gift-wrapped. He opened it. Inside the box was a new one, even nicer than the one he had lost.

23. She had changed. She looked different to him. Odd, but she looked like him. It finally dawned on him what had happened— she had replaced herself with a mirror. So he did the same thing. Replaced himself with a mirror. Then he stood back and watched.

24. "How is it outside?" she asked.

"I don't know," he said. "Let me look." He went to the window. "It's sunny," he said and walked away.

She went to look for herself. "It's not sunny," she said. "It's cloudy."

After she had walked away from the window he went back to take another look. "You're crazy," he said. "It's sunny." And he walked away.

She went back to the window. It was cloudy.

This went on for some time. They took turns looking out the window. Every time he looked it was sunny, every time she looked it was cloudy. They finally decided that the only way to settle the matter once and for all was for both of them to look out the window at the same time. So they did. It was night.

25. They had a famous painter do a double portrait. When he had finished, the painter asked, "Well, how do you like it?"

"It's a good likeness of him," she said, "but it doesn't look anything like me."

"And how do you feel about it?" the painter asked him.

"Well," he replied, "I think it's an excellent likeness of her, but I must say it doesn't look a bit like me."

The painter smiled and said, "I painted you as you see each other."

SUSAN DAITCH

Camera Obscura

1. Images of Panic

Dale Arden didn't look Flash Gordon in the eye. She focused somewhere off the page, perhaps on the control panel. She was sick of wars, bored stiff with the constant chase. Nearly always it was Ming the Merciless. Ming the Merciless stuck to her intergalactic trail because he didn't give up, wouldn't accept defeat, and his thirst for revenge had reached the proportions of obsession many frames ago. So far she'd always had some kind of edge, taking him by surprise, episode after episode. Spinning off into ever-deeper space it occurred to Dale that some day a caper might come along and she'd falter. Just when he's about to slice with the red hot pincers or fill the last few inches of the water tank, just at that moment when there's no hope at all, her stores of agility and guile might turn mirage. Even Professor Zarkov, on whose nerves of a practical rational fiber they often depended, even he would be shocked, if not extremely sorry. Dale Arden turned pacifist. It was 1939. Diana Palmer, in love with the Phantom, sleeps alone dreaming pesky, censored scenes only to have them metamorphose into something unsatisfying and mundane. The Phantom will never marry her. She wakes up. Molly Day, girl detective; Sala, villainess, queen of outlaws; in the dominion of Cockaigne Princess Narda tries to murder Mandrake; Lil' de Vrille gave up her role as the Vampire Queen extortionist—her love for Jungle Jim rearranging her crooked heart like the spirit of a Calvinist missionary among easy converts, Incas maybe. Grace Powers says, "Men! Putty!" Blondie, Olive Oyl, Tillie the Toiler; I rolled the cartoons into a tube and held the phony telescope up to my left eye, squinting as if focusing the view through smeared print.

2. Projection of Murder

In the apartment building across the street a man and a woman seemed to be rehearsing lines for a play. The woman turned dramatically and appeared to address the audience with an emotion which approached stage anguish. Her theater was empty except for me at my window and anyone else in the Sherwood Arms with a north view, a sharp eye, and an empty afternoon. The man put his script under his arm, came up behind her, took her elbows in his hands as if to say, "Let's go through this part again," or perhaps what he mouthed was a line from the folded script. The woman was dressed like Burma from *Terry and the Pirates*, shirt unbuttoned, long slit skirt. My survey has always been random, but the actress across the street seemed as concerned with her costume as Sheena, Queen of the Jungle. I can't tell when they're pretending or when she's really angry. She throws a drink, collapses into tears, then picks up a script. Her partner pulled a gun. Within the perimeters of the strip some characters freely lived their lives half-clothed. There are those who might interpret the neighbors' exhibitionism differently. A woman walking around her apartment half-dressed might be a sign of high-class prostitution. I continued to pursue their rehearsals episodically. The actor bore a resemblance to Terry's friend Pat Ryan, but in some scenes he was like Prince Valiant in a white tuxedo. The frieze running around their building included stone satyrs, fruit, and musical instruments.

3. Architectural Mistake

The Sherwood Arms was not a bad place to live. My apartment repeated the lobby's Gothic theme. Pointed arches, mass-produced somewhere in the Bronx, were multiplied over and over but in a manner which spelled out: Manhattan Gothic. The medieval tone was run-down and interrupted by the appearance of transient tenants, the sort who would never have crossed the threshold of a cathedral, and by the repairmen who usually came once a month to fix the elevator, and replace light bulbs in the shape of candle flames in the lobby. The elevator doors on each floor bore paintings of heraldic shields in shades of red and brown, swords and arrows pointed toward the up and down buttons. On some floors they had been entirely painted over with a cheap copper-colored paint. Illegible names, telephone numbers and often vaguely obscene writing were scrawled across some of the shields. My floor was fairly clean. The windows in each apartment had narrow diamond panes, but as the leading grew faulty, the landlord no longer bothered with individual panes. He would replace the whole window with a single sheet of glass so there were fewer and fewer of the original. Each minor labor-saving device further nullified or contradicted the anachronistic medieval bits that did remain.

In my apartment, as if to insist on modern times, I kept a Bakelite radio in each room, which was no financial strain as there were only three of them.

The couple across the street played with a prop gun. They read their lines, struggled over it, suddenly looked stunned. It must have gone off, a bullet pierced a painting. They walked over to the picture and put their hands over the spot, but perhaps their disbelief was part of the plot. I turned on the radio.

4. Expiration

"An hour ago the ten-ton diving bell disappeared from view. As it sank to the bottom of the ocean, we've been spending anxious minutes waiting in a row boat as close to the submarine's location as the Coast Guard will allow. Just a few minutes before we came on the air, the immense bell broke the water's surface . . . . Men aboard the *Falcon* are maneuvering it toward the stem of the ship by means of a long pole. They seem to have it in the desired position now, two men are astride the bell, working on the hatch cover in an attempt to unscrew the bolts which keep the hatch sealed against the sea and the tremendous water pressure two hundred and fifty feet below the surface.

"One of the men is rising from his crouched position now, and the men aboard the rescue ship are leaning tensely over the side."

The submarine *Squalus* had begun to take in water from an open induction valve and had sunk somewhere in the Atlantic. The rescue operation, designed by navy engineers, was slow and uncertain, and the submarine was gradually filling with water. Cables, chambers, water ballast, suction cups, changes in air pressure. Only a few men at a time could come up in the bell. How do they decide who goes up each time? Some would be patient, gamble on navy technology, let others up first. Some might fight to grab a space in the bell-shaped vessel as it makes each slow trip from the pigboat to the rescue ship. A cable might tangle and snap, just seventy-five feet left to go. Men trapped all over the place, running out of oxygen, water trickling in. The ocean has the relentless power of the majority. You can't tell it to take a break and come back in twenty minutes.

". . . the hatch cover of the diving bell is open. They're reaching down inside the bell now . . . and there's the first man's head."*

Going quietly berserk knowing the sea wasn't waiting for the ingenious but slow invention of navy engineers, if I were down in the *Squalus* would patience, and what I thought was heroic, generous behavior, win over anxiety to get out? Slowly, section after section of the submarine filled with water. I didn't want to think about the last man left waiting for the rescue bell in neither idle nor self-imposed solitude.

* Columbia Broadcasting Service, 1939

A shortwave radio transmitter operating at 2190 kilocycles makes this broadcast possible.

It often seemed useless to leave the Sherwood Arms, and if it were not for the necessity of paying rent, I would have remained as trapped, altruistically and suicidally letting others into the rescue bell first.

5. Working and Leaving

Sometimes I thought the actors across the street were imitating me, though they didn't appear to observe anyone but each other. On occasions when I tried to find a job, I returned home to find them dressed in costumes of miners and farmers. Unless they were preparing for yet another performance, I was sure that they couldn't be engaged in professions like these in the middle of New York. My neighbors were real actors. I mean they seemed to earn a living at it and never had to look for other kinds of work as far as I could tell. I never saw them standing in lines or selling their possessions on the street.

One evening after filling out forms that I knew would never lead to employment, I was able to sneak into a theater where *True Confessions* was showing. Carole Lombard played a writer whose husband, Fred MacMurray, was a scrupulously honest lawyer, therefore, they were starving. He didn't want his wife to work, but she did slip out of the house one day and go for a job interview. The job turned out to involve "being nice" to a rich man who lived in a mansion. Sit closer, closer still, take dictation, take it sitting on my lap. She ran out of the house, but in those few minutes someone murdered the wealthy philanderer, and Carole Lombard was framed for the murder. The case looked hopeless. Her husband didn't realize she was innocent and argued her case on the basis of self-defense. The lie began to take root. Hinged on it all her dreams of success were to come true. A drunken member of the court audience told her that she'd fry for the murder. He knew what he was talking about. He'd been attending trials for years, a regular roach who thrived on litigation. She was acquitted, wrote a book about her trial, became famous, did lecture tours. As a result, everyone wanted to publish her stories. I knew no one rich enough or whose life was so great a target that any connection I might have to their assassination could get me a book contract. Whenever Carole Lombard had an idea, she pressed her tongue against her cheek so it stuck out.

The actress twirled the toy gun around her finger and balanced a glass on her stomach as she lay on a couch. My lights were off, my clothes were arranged on a chair as if the chair were occupied by a very flat person. The actor straightened his tie in the mirror. He might have been going out but didn't leave. He slouched in an armchair. I could see empty glasses lying in several places. To be honest, they spent a lot of time behaving like victims of narcoleptic attacks. Perhaps they were out of work, slept through rehearsals, no longer cared about acting.

I sat in my apartment with the Phantom, Ming the Merciless and the radio as if there were no tomorrows, but then I had cause to fret. The actors across the street began to rearrange their furniture. Sometimes it looked as if they were packing, then unpacking, then putting boxes near the door again. Whether they had been evicted, were moving out, or were just going on a trip, I hadn't a clue. Perhaps they were only separating from each other. In the next frame, like Dale Arden, they escaped at the last minute.

DARIUS JAMES

Negrophobia

Two scenes from a screenplay

EPISODE I

FADE IN:

INT. KITCHEN—MORNING

CLOSE ON: AUNT JEMIMA's chunky brown face beaming on a cylinder-shaped box of grits.

PULL BACK: and reveal a hefty black arm stirring a cauldron of grits.

A series of short, farting bursts as grits boil and bubble.

The stirring ladle is lifted from the cauldron. Pinched by the tip of its tail, a live MOUSE is dangled over the wisps of steam rising from the cauldron and dropped in. The mouse squeals, paddles frantically, vomits blood and dies. The ladle is placed back in the cauldron and stirring resumes. The dead mouse sinks beneath the surface of grits.

(OS) Voice is heard as camera PULLS BACK

When 'at boy gwine learn his se'f som' sense? Ah done tol'
'lat boy messin' wif' dem whyte gals gwine a'git 'im keel.

MAID comes into view. It is her voice we've been hearing. An
open pancake box, a splattered mixing bowl and fish entrails are
seen on nearby counter. The Maid is a monstrous mammy-sized
cookie jar with doughy animal features and crazed incandescent
eyes. Her nappy bleached-blonde Afro is a crown of spiky thorns
matted with sweat and splashed with splots of Day-Glo color. Her
face and arms are splotched with large leaf-like patches of missing
melanin. The twirl of brown and pink stripes on her left arm
resemble the markings of a tiger's coat. A pair of mascara lobster-
claws wings her eyes. The Maid stirs her brew of grits as she talks
on the telephone.

MAID

Jus' don' lissen . . . head hard as a rock. He kno'd what
happin' t'his Unca Lemmie down in Georgia wif' dat yung
whyte gal . . . yas chile, fool crackas strung 'im up, gutted
'im like a pig 'n bar-b-que'd his ass . . . smackin' dey lips 'n
talkin' 'bout *gimme 'notha dem greasy nigga ribs* . . . Ah
don' kno', you tell me what dat ol' snagga mouf' buck-eye
coon want wif' a yung one? Broke-dick nigga couldn't get
his dick hard since 1926! Saw dat yung whyte gal's pussy—
HARD DICK F'DAZE!! Ol' wrinkle-ass *HUFFIN 'N
HUNCHIN'* nigga what said he only meant to rub it f'luck
'cause dat whyte gal's pussy *look jus' like d'top of a nigga's
head!* Chicken rustlin' rascal. Nah dat Weefee ridin' 'round
wif dat carload o' whyte gals, can't tell dat nigga nuffin'.
He be talkin' 'bout slick skull game, how he hard on his
ho's, keep a big roll in his pocket 'n d'rest ob dat ol' *okey-
doke!* Ah oughts t'go out dere mysefs 'n take a switch to
dat citified country nigga's—GREAT GUGAMUGA!!

The Maid's eyes are disks of surprise. Her mouth an *O* of wonder.

Bubbles enters kitchen and sits at breakfast table. She stares at the pile of pancakes placed on the plate in front of her. Hundreds of FISH EYES fried inside stare back.

The Maid glares at the ovals on Bubbles' face.

With mock innocence, Bubbles smiles. She reaches into her jacket's side pocket and eats, one by one, a handful of human-shaped chocolate figurines. Webs of masticated chocolate pop in her mouth.

                    MAID (Into phone)
　　Lucille, I'ma hasta call y'back later.

Maid hangs telephone back on wall.

                    MAID
MISS BUBBAS BRASIL! WHAT IS DAT DEVILISH MESS CAKED ON YO' FACE?!!

                    BUBBLES
Magically converging uteri to equalize the balance of negative and positive energies in my karma.

                    MAID
Mah' 'uta—*wha?*

                    BUBBLES
Warpaint.

                    MAID
Why can't you dream up sum'in prac'tica', like, how ah can hit d'numba?

                    BUBBLES
What's a white girl to do in a school full of jigaboos?

                    MAID
Mind her business. Yo' parents spent all dat money sendin' you off to fancy private schools 'n whatchoo do? *Getcha hot little boll-dagga ass throad out!* And then you end up in a crazyhouse fo' rich *DOPE FIENDS!* Face it, yo' is jus' gon haf'ta put up wid dem niggas.

Bubbles wrinkles her nose.

> **BUBBLES**
> But they're *gross* and they *spit*.

A half-eaten *niggerbaby* spits from her mouth.

> **MAID**
> Spit back at 'em . . .

> **BUBBLES**
> But you don't know what it's like! Girls yank my hair and
> guys yank my tits! That place is a fucking monkey house!
> (Eating another niggerbaby)
> *Jigaboos!*

Bubbles folds her arms across her breasts and pouts.

> **MAID**
> Lookie here, MISS WHYTE 'N MIGHTY! In dis' kitchen,
> whyte is right if it can kick THREE HUNDRED 'N SIXTY
> POUNDS OF SWEATIN' BLACK ASS!!! Ah don' takes
> t'you 'ferrin' t'my peepus as *jigaboos*. You makes us out
> t'sound like we be hidin' in d'bushes affa dark wif' our teef'
> shinin' 'n shit.

> **BUBBLES**
> Coons hide in the bushes with their teeth shining.

Maid lifts ladle dripping with hot grits and tries to whomp Bubbles
up side d'haid but misses.

> **MAID**
> Don't sass mouf' me!

> **BUBBLES**
> Well it's true . . .

MAID

Nah dat we is no longa cullid, we is whatchoo calls Neo-African Americans —hostages misplaced in time, captives of a racist his'tre 'n a oppressed peepus dissolvin' in d'stomach acids of whyte Amerika, *d'cause of so much bad breffs!*

BUBBLES

Monkey chatter! I'm oppressed! But you wouldn't understand that—*you were never white and pretty!*

MAID

'N you was never black 'n broke!

BUBBLES

Thank god! I don't know what I'd do without my mane of golden fairy-tale curls.

MAID

'N you wonder why dem niggas be bustin' yo' behind all d'time.

BUBBLES

I don't wonder. I know.

MAID

If'n you knows so much, what put d'idea in yo'head t'put dat mess on yo' face in d'first place?

BUBBLES

One of your books.

Maid's eyes spark with paranoia.

MAID

Which books?

BUBBLES

The creepy ones.

The Maid's voice builds in increasing degrees of anger.

MAID

Which "creepy ones"?

BUBBLES

The ones you buy from the Puerto Ricans. "How to Cause Constipation," "Protection from the Evil Eye," "Black Herman's Book of Shrunken Talking Heads" . . .

MAID

YOU BEEN MESSIN' IN MY MOJOS!!! I tol' you 'bout bein' in my books! Dems my sacred books 'n not fo' d'eyes o' whyte folks! I'ma whips d'hoodoos on you fo' sho'!

With her fingers curled and clutching, the Maid leaps for Bubbles' throat and freezes. Her eyes spin in dizzy circles, turning up in her head until only the whites are visible. Her tongue contorts, flopping one way and then the other. Her forehead erupts with beads of sweat. Her head goosenecks back and forth. Her shoulders hunch and jerk.

MAID

I'ma hang d'gris-gris 'bove you' do'! Snakes gwine crawl 'cross yo' flo'! D'rats gwine howl 'n blood gwine run down yo' jo'! Yo' body gwine bust out in nasty so's! Yo' ass gwine shrivel up 'n you aints gwine shits no mo'!

Bubbles' eyes are circles of awe, an expression of surprise, not fear. She has never seen such a loon coon.

The Maid slithers into snake dance. She convulses with spasms, foams at the mouth and rips her clothing. Clusters of sweat cling to her armpit hair. Slinging fish-eye pancakes frisbee style, she improvises James Brown songs, intermixing Bruce Lee Kung-Fu cat cries and lines from *Gone With the Wind* ("Ah noze all 'bout birfin' babies, Miz Scarlett—jus' fetch me dat rusty coat hanger."). Twirling in a daze, the Maid cackles and collapses on the floor with her tongue lolling from her mouth.

Bubbles stands, walks over to the prostrate Maid and kneels. The Maid pants like a young slut. Her eyes flutter open.

*NAH MARCH UPSTAIRS 'N WASH YO' FACE 'FORE
AH WEAR YO' HINDPOTS OUT WIF" DIS' HERE
SPOON O' HOT HOMINY!!*

Bubbles leaps to her feet and dashes from the kitchen. The Maid
laughs long, loud and hysterical.

DOLLY IN for CLOSE SHOT of MAID'S FACE

DISSOLVE

FADE OUT

END EPISODE I

EPISODE II

FADE IN:

INT. SUBWAY CAR—DAY

Train's loud locomotive *rattle*.

BUBBLES hunched into a ball on the metal bench, her feet curled
beneath her. The rattle and rumble rocks her bod. She is seated
between a NURSE and a WINO. The nurse is fat and black and
the wino is black and babbling. The wino is dressed in the discarded
costuming he's found in the theater district's trash bins. Feathers
and sequins float to the floor. He laughs, slaps his thighs and
smokes invisible cigarettes. His manner is that of the rich, successful and famous on the TV talk show circuit. He believes he is
being interviewed by Merv Griffin.

WINO

I was makin' big money in 1920—*$250 a week!* Know why?
I'm the *original* Little Rascal! *Sunshine Sammy!* I was

before Farina, Stymie, Buckwheat—any o' them has-beens!
Now I make $50,000 a night, and you wanna know some-
thin', Merv? I'm a bigger draw than Elvis ever was!

The wino impersonates Elvis Presley.

> WINO
> When I first startin' singin', they said I sound like a nigger.
> Now I play two shows a night at the Pearly Gates. Betcha
> y'all think God looks like Santa Claus in a nightshirt, right?
> Uh-uh. He looks like Liberace.

The wino drops the Elvis persona.

> WINO
> I'm back-slappin' buddies with Dino, Frank, Sammy, Jerry
> *and his crippled children!* They call me *Mr. Entertainment*
> himself! Why, I taught Scatman Crothers everything he
> knows!

The wino annoys the nurse seated on Bubbles' right. The nurse
looks at the wino and rolls her eyes in disgust. Annoyance flickers
across the faces of the other PASSENGERS in the subway car.
The wino turns to Bubbles and speaks.

> WINO
> Y'kno', we didn't have pussy when I was a boy. That's right.
> Pussy hadn't been discovered yet. Pussy was discovered in
> 1827 by Massa Johnson in a cave down in Mississippi. He'd
> gone out quail huntin' and there it was—Pussy. Sittin' right
> up there in a cave. Laughin'.

Bubbles tries to ignore the wino. Her body seems to shrink smaller
in size as the wino grows more obnoxious.

> WINO
> I don't know what the hell it is, but let's grease it down
> and fuck it anyways!

The train stops. Bubbles looks over her shoulder and out the window. Passengers file into the subway car, filling the seats and

jamming the aisle. Bubbles is suddenly conscious of the fact she is the only white in the subway car and begins to feel her first wave of anxiety. Cattle-crammed bodies sparkle with perspiration. Bubbles wrinkles her nose at the thick negro smell.

A conga-drum-carrying ALBINO enters and situates himself by the sliding doors on the left side of the car's far end. His skin is the urine hue of unflavored gelatin. His eyes rabbit pink. His Afro nicotine yellow. He wears billowing bulb-bottomed pants and silk slippers with curved toes. Also a skullcap and African robes. His palms paddle conga skins.

> ALBINO
> Snake drums call you from the devil's land. May the snake take your spirits, and you rear up like the cobra and strike. Then, my bruthas and sistas, you shall dance, you shall dance . . .

An angered VOICE (OS) shouts:

> VOICE
> *Shut up wid dem drums*, you funny-lookin' 'Rabian Nights nigga! I gots Thundabird poundin' in my head dis' mornin'!

The albino paddles conga skins.

> ALBINO
> This is no "Arabian Nights," brutha. This is Amerika the Treacherous! And my name is Abdul! I'm an Inner-City Shaman, a Ministrel of Mau-Mau Metaphysics and a Pop Poet of Oppressed People's Propaganda!!!

> ANGRY VOICE
> Ooooo pleez, nigga, shut up, my head. Yo, anybody know what color classification dis' nigga's complexion qualify for?

> ANOTHER VOICE
> I don't know, but if you rub his 'fro, I betcha a genie fly out in a cloud o'reefer smoke and grant you three wishes!

Passengers laugh loudly. Though embarrassed, the albino continues his conga pounding.

DOMESTICS, FACTORY WORKERS, STREET HUSTLERS, MARICONES, JUNKIE TRANSVESTITES and other SLUM DWELLERS of increasing strangeness enter the subway car. They converge on Bubbles from all sides, enveloping her in a host of ghoulish faces. Bubbles is enwrapped by a smothering fear, suffocating in a density of darkies. *Bloodshot eyes, broad nostrils, and fat, hungry lips* anticipate the taste of her sweet honkie meat. A MONTAGE of faces stab her consciousness in quick succession, fragmentary images congealing into a cubistic portrait of urban paranoia, evoking a freakish, low-lit eerieness: a MINISTER with no face, peeling skin covers the hollows of his skull where his eyes, nose, and mouth should be. Gimpy RETARDS push through the sea of the earth's crazed and wretched. Drooling MONGOLOIDS, PINHEADS and deformed DWARVES shamble toward Bubbles and cluster around, making a pathetic sound somewhere between a pant and a whine. Hands fondle her breasts and stroke her hair.

Bubbles shuts her eyes in horror.

Upon opening her eyes, she finds a testicle drooping from an open fly. She looks up. A JUNKIE gripping an overhead strap, adrift in the Land of Heavy Nod. He is unaware of either self or surroundings. Dangling dead weight swinging to the train's rock and rumble.

The Junkie's pelvis thrusts back and forth in Bubbles' face, locomotives and conga-drum thuddings in sync with the junkie's pelvic thrustings.

Bubbles overhears a conversation between two members of an uptown street gang. There is a fervent religious intensity in their voices. TEEN 2 is an Amen-sycophant, tapping his cane on the floor each time he speaks.

TEEN 1

. . . wall to wall whities. Me, up north, in Maine, with wall to wall whities. Me and this otha brutha. And he didn't even count. Was one of those upwardly mo'*bile* niggas of the boushie boogahood.

TEEN 2

An androided nigga.

Taps cane twice.

TEEN 1

Right. Manufactured in one of whitie's nigga factories. The original prototype for nigga-baby candies. Popped hot from a monster mold.

TEEN 2

A Klingon nigga.

Taps cane twice.

TEEN 1

A Klingon nigga. The Coon from Planet X. Spoke an alien tongue. Jus' me 'n dis' out-of-tune buffoon 'mongst wall-to-wall whities. As a gen-u-wine, card-carryin', jittabuggin' jigaboo, honkies made it a point to check me out. Ofay bitches was constantly rubbin' my kinks 'n talkin' 'bout, *"It does feel like a Brillo pad!!"* In the mornin's, when I be takin' my showers, I was pullin' fistfulls of blond pussy hair out my crotch . . .
    (Grips penis and rubs, knees shaking)
Brutha, I was *gunnin'!*

TEEN 2

Gunnin' the Great White Bitch!

Taps cane twice.

TEEN 1

Gunnin' the Great White Bitch. I swore the total annihilation of the entire white race and anything left with the faintest trace of demon honkie scent *for the bitch drove me mad!* Was nuthin' a nigga could relate to. A world without James Brown 45s.

No James Brown 45s.

Taps cane twice.

No *Jet* magazines!

No greasy collard greens!

Teen 1 & 2 look Bubbles in the eyes. SLOW DOLLY to CLOSE SHOT of Bubbles' face.

Jus' m'black ass 'n a afro pick!

TEEN 2 taps cane twice. Echo and FADE TO BLACKS.

END EPISODE II

TAMA JANOWITZ

Case History #179: Tina

Tina lived with her boyfriend in his luxurious apartment on Madison Avenue. Her boyfriend was a well-known art dealer who had inherited an illustrious gallery from his father; their apartment was filled with valuable paintings and art deco furnishings in ebony and red lacquer.

Her boyfriend was very absent-minded and this drove Tina crazy. No matter how many times she reminded him to pick up something from the store, to turn off the stove before leaving the apartment, or to check the address book for the address before they went to the party, somehow he always forgot.

"Tina," he would say, "what the hell do you worry for so much, you're like an old lady."

Tina was high-strung, screechy as a violin, with hair like twisted licorice. She had been raised by her nervous grandmother who could never leave the house without returning moments later to make sure the iron was unplugged. Even though Tina had hated this and had resolved never to be so nervous, this trait—possibly genetic—had rubbed off on her. Sometimes, while sitting in the movie theater, Tina would have an overwhelming urge to tap her boyfriend on the shoulder and say, "Are you sure you remembered to shut off the water in the bathtub before we left?" But she knew her boyfriend was not a reassuring type and would tell her to knock it off, or say that if she kept on this way he would leave her. She knew if that ever happened she would die.

But even if she did check all the appliances before going out, to make sure they were off, she always had a nagging suspicion that she hadn't. Due to this nervousness Tina's life was not pleasant, although there had never once been a household accident which might have given her cause for alarm.

The curious thing was that her boyfriend was always getting into accidents. He would open the refrigerator, for example, and a bottle of ketchup would leap out and hit him in the forehead. Once he fell down the spiral staircase and was in a cast for six weeks. He always blamed these accidents on Tina—she was the last person to use the ketchup, she had waxed the floor at the top of the stairs—but Tina couldn't really take his complaints very seriously. "You've always been accident-prone," she said. "I wish you'd be more careful. I'd die if anything happened to you."

After he sliced open his foot on one of Tina's razors that she had left in the tub he told her he could never marry her. Though he was fond of her, he said, her perpetual nagging drove him crazy, all in all she wasn't sane, and he never felt he could really trust her. "Of course, I don't mind going on this way for the time being," he explained, "but I think I should be honest and tell you that at this point I'm thinking about having an affair with another woman."

Tina wept for hours. She told her boyfriend how much she adored him, how he meant everything to her, and that he would never find anyone to care for him as much. "If you make me leave I'll kill myself," she said.

"Knock it off, Tina," he said. "Subject closed. I'll help you find a new apartment."

A few nights later her boyfriend had a cold. Tina decided to attend a party, to which they had both been invited, without him. Her boyfriend lay in bed, smoking cigarettes and blowing his nose. Finally he drifted off to sleep. Before going out, Tina carefully emptied the ashtray into the wastebasket and cleaned up the tissues and empty soup bowls.

She had a fine time at the party—some guy flirted with her—and she realized that perhaps if she began to spend time with other men her boyfriend might treat her more seriously.

When she got home the ambulance was carrying off some charred remains. Something—possibly the wastebasket where she had thrown the ashes and tissues—had caught on fire, and her dozing boyfriend had not woken up in time.

Tina felt so terrible she had a nervous breakdown. When she was released from the hospital, a year later, she no longer wanted to kill herself: the doctors explained that while it was true she was responsible, she did not have to go on punishing herself.

Though she agreed, out of guilt she became a bag person. She lived on the streets; at night she slept on top of subway gratings. All of her belongings were in paper bags. Later a magazine featured her on the cover as part of a story on street people. "How do you feel?" the reporter asked her.

"Well, frankly, I'm quite happy," Tina said. Her pale face was red and chapped from the cold, and some old rags were tied around her head and hands. "I mean," she said, "at least I don't have to worry about whether or not I left the stove on."

But the reporter did not understand this at all, and merely wrote in his article how terrible it was that nowadays people were simply medicated and released from mental institutions without being prepared for reality. He gave Tina ten dollars, and after the article appeared she was offered a job cleaning the women's bathroom in Grand Central Station. But Tina found this job to be so difficult, so anxiety-provoking—there were so many people to check up on, after all, to make sure they had washed their hands properly and yet were not using the facilities to brush their teeth or change their clothes—that a short time later she returned to the streets, where she disappeared from sight.

GARY INDIANA

I Am Candy Jones

I am Candy Jones. I am also Mildred Huxley. This is our story. Six months ago at Plato's Retreat I met, and fell in love with, my current husband, Dick Bridgely, an animal psychiatrist of international repute. Until shortly before our marriage, I was employed as an accountant at the Bea Lin Korean Vegetables Company, known worldwide for its miraculously large produce and "all you can eat for a dollar" salad bars. I had been working for the shadowy Bea Lin for six years, spot-checking vegetable and salad oil receipts throughout America and Europe. I was well paid and owned the cooperative apartment which I still maintain, though I now share Dick's townhouse in the East Sixties. I had always been a happy girl, came from a happy family, and had always led a happy life, as far as I was aware. But now I'm getting ahead of myself. Perhaps I should take the reader back down memory lane a few steps before I explain how I was brainwashed and tortured by the CIA, forced to commit acts of unspeakable evil, and practically killed so I wouldn't talk.

I still remember our ranch-style home in Reno, Nevada, out there on the desert near the testing range. My dad, Chuck Jones, had dreamed his whole life of living in the ozone-enriched dry air at the periphery of Reno. My mother, Cindy Jones, was a beautiful woman, tall, with large hair and eyes that spoke volumes despite her quiet manner. She was mute, but as a child I never knew. My father, you see, had had his own vocal cords severed in a bizarre car accident shortly before my birth. I had no brothers or sisters, and because my parents had no friends and our home was in a remote area, I learned to talk by watching television. I know that some will find the speechlessness of my family life shocking or dismal. But it was neither shocking nor dismal. I adored my parents and their wordless ways. I should probably explain that my father was a millionaire inventor. He had invented an inexpensive method of producing weapons-grade uranium for the U.S. Government and held four original patents on advance detonation devices. He had once been a gregarious man, but something, I never knew what, had happened shortly before I was born, a dispute of some kind with certain bureaucrats at Livermore Laboratories. Whatever it was, my dad was damned mad about it, and had even agreed to go on a radio talk show in Los Angeles to tell his side of the story, but it was not to be. On his way to the radio studio, driving on the San Bernardino Freeway, my father's Volkswagen was rear-ended by a large vehicle and sent spinning and hurtling, or tumbling, through space. The other vehicle continued on and to this day we will never know who was operating it. As for my father, he would never speak again.

My mother was the bright sunlight in all three of our lives: she cooked and cleaned incessantly.

"Candy," she would write in my composition book, "come out to the kitchen, I've prepared something marvelous for you!"

I still get a little clog in my windpipe when I recall my mother's exclamation points. And there, on the vermillion formica tabletop, would be a vast or huge cherry, apple, or other kind of delicious pie. By this time I could talk fluently, and was ever jabbering away.

"Golly, Mom, this pie is scrumptious!" I would squeal after

chewing a delicate forkful. "It's super-delicious and nutritious!"

Mom would wipe bleary tears from her very large eyes, sniffle and shake her head with happiness. Then Dad would bound into the room, his appetite hearty from a busy morning of feeding the snakes.

"Heavens to Betsy, Dad, try a piece of this apple-delicious pie that Mom made!"

The Chuck and Cindy Jones Reptile Ranch was the center of my early life: feeding the baby rattlers with an eyedropper, mixing protein meal into the Gila monster's mash, and when I was old enough, extracting venom for the research laboratory in Oxnard, California, our principal customer. There, the venom would be processed into life-saving vaccines, and sometimes for other useful purposes. I loved our rattlesnakes. They were always getting into mischief and playing little pranks. Though they finally cost my mother and father their lives, I still believe it was an accident and a case of human error which could have been avoided, if only the man from the Oxnard laboratory had listened to my father's written words and not insisted on taking two of our largest and most unpredictable ones into the guest bedroom that night to study their habits. Though he himself miraculously escaped harm, the rattlers slithered into my parents' bedroom, excited by some unknown source. At least death came to them quick. I was not in the house at the time, for this occurred when I had already entered accounting school and resided in California. Otherwise, I too might not be here to tell the tale.

Romance hit me for the first time in California. His name was Jeff and he drove an adorable MG. Fortunately Jeff was by my side when the news of my parents' untimely deaths arrived by telegram.

"Candy, honey," Jeff tried to comfort me as best he could, cradling me gently in his evenly tanned arms. "Death gets the best of us one way or the other. Just take comfort that they went fast, and there wasn't any pain."

"Oh, but Jeff," I sobbed. "Today would have been their fiftieth anniversary. Mom would have baked a beautiful pie, and Dad would've put Aqua Velva behind his ears before he gave her her present, a beautiful gold watch."

I happened to know at the time that my father had been planning to surprise Mom with a gold watch. Ironic that a gold watch would come to play a very different, sinister role in the life of yours truly. But life is ironic, as my husband Dick likes to say, though both of us are hoping to keep irony at arm's length for a while after what I am going to tell you eventually.

It was the 60s, and you know what they were. I was blonde, busty, and bored in accounting school, though I hasten to say I was by no means miserable. Au contraire, Miss Popularity would only begin to describe the way heads would turn when I walked through the corridors of the Samuel Fuller School of Accounting on La Cienega Boulevard. We were not far from Hollywood High, and a list of hunky dudes I dated then would make *Seventeen* look like *Good Housekeeping*. I'm not bragging but complaining: I couldn't keep the boys off me, and what was even worse, I was becoming radicalized.

That's right. Me, Candy Jones, or rather I, Candy Jones, bee-hive princess, was caught up in the whirl of events we now think of as the 60s. I went on marches. I signed petitions. I demonstrated. Now when I look back on it all I still think it was the right thing to do at the time. But the tragedy is, you see, that when this kind of idea comes over me now, I'm never quite sure that it isn't Mildred talking. Mildred who has my big hair, my large eyes, my breasts and all the rest of all that. Mildred whose voice is different than mine; I have heard on the tape-recorder recordings my husband, Dick Bridgely, has made of Mildred's voice coming out of my, Candy Jones's, mouth. Mildred would never go on marches or make statements against the government because the government is exactly who programmed her to kill, lie, dump poison in hotel water supplies. But now I'm getting ahead of myself again. I just wanted to point out that even though Mildred was created by the government, whenever I get excited, even over a good cause, there is always that doubt whether it is me, Candy Jones, experiencing excitement, or if it is Mildred, Mildred again, bringing the body we share up to a fever pitch that "Candy" has never known.

Oh, Dick, I'm afraid. I can't talk anymore.

-

-

-

The incredible story you have begun to hear, or read, is true. I would never have believed this story unless it had brushed against my own life in the most direct manner possible, and still, upon occasion, when I listen to the eerie revelations of "Mildred," my wife Candy Jones's alter ego, implanted by the Central Intelligence Agency, my mind literally reels, I gasp, I hyperventilate in something like pure horror.

My name is Dick Bridgely, and chances are you've seen my name, or seen my guest appearances on the Johnny Carson show. I am, of course, an authority on the behavior of animals in captivity, and have published many well-known books on the psychology of domestic pets. Until my marriage to Candy Jones, whose incredible ordeal you are reading about, my life, like most lives, was a fairly ordinary one, despite my international renown. I went to my office on Park Avenue every day when not called away to some world conference on cat paranoia and the like. And, like most people, I always felt that there were some disturbing aspects of the U.S. Government I seldom heard about, but that basically the conservative sweep of recent years was just part of the old American yin-yang syndrome, causing a few miscellaneous injustices and even here and there a case of out-and-out political repression. But hell, I figured, any day now that fickle American public will want long hair and love beads and Up The Revolution all over again. I mean, just look at the clothes on these Fundamentalists, it's spooky, and with MTV and cable every Baptist in the country is bopping to the beat and watching suck-off porn where his neighbors can't see him. That's bound to shake up the shit.

Little did I know.

I'll never forget the night I met Candy Jones. Because the buxom, black-haired girl who was rimming me, and the German beauty who was grinding her pussy into my tongue, both felt my muscles stiffen. My cock, which is eleven inches long when it's hard, seemed to grow two inches as I stared at the corn-fed, innocent-looking blonde girl who had wandered into our alcove at Plato's Retreat. Gently, but firmly, I detached my anus from the black-haired girl's probing tongue, my own tongue from the imperious Teuton's clit.

"I'm having a personal crisis," I told them. "I'm in love."

"A million assholes wandering around and I gotta pick yours," sneered the raven-haired lovely.

"Plenty more cunt-eaters where he came from," the Prussian temptress consoled her, leading her away. And then I was alone with Candy Jones.

"Fuck me," she said, simply. But her head turned slightly away in embarrassment. I could tell she found the environment a little distasteful, and that she wasn't used to satisfying her needs in quite such direct ways.

"Why don't you begin by eating my dick," I whispered. "That way I can look at your beautiful ass while you suck me off."

"That's quite a hard-on," Candy breathed, sinking to her knees and working her moist, perfect lips around the head of my throbbing penis—but ever so gently, as if it contained the very juice of the gods.

That night I fucked Candy Jones for something like three hours. My nuts ached the whole next day and I couldn't get her out of my mind. She had given me her phone number but we all know what that's worth. Half the time they're phony numbers, and the other half it's I don't remember. But those three hours with my prick inside her slavering clam had convinced me that this was the woman of my dreams.

Boy, talk about behavior.

Then we were married. Not just happily but blissfully. I believe it is rare that a man and a woman experience the kind of happiness that Candy and I knew in those first weeks of married life. The little things as well as the big things. We daydreamed together about a vacation in Hawaii. Candy's perfect eye supervised the remodeling of my three-story townhouse, one of the truly enviable properties in Manhattan's booming real-estate network. My equity in the place compared to what it was worth would've made anybody's eyes water and their mouth drool. We thought we had it all, and we were on our way to getting a whole lot more of it.

Until the night Mildred came to call.

I still feel like somebody spit an ice cube into my rectum when I think of the first night that Mildred made herself known to me.

-

-

-

"I loved the way you ate my asshole out *after* I made you come," I was telling Candy. Or so I thought.

"You're all asshole," snarled an alien voice, sending the hairs on the back of my neck into full erection.

"Candy, what's wrong?"

"I'm not Candy."

I turned to look at her. And came closer to a coronary than a man of my age and near-perfect physical condition normally comes. The woman beside me on the huge bed of our primarily dark-green-with-white-trim bedroom was not, could not have been, anyone like Candy Jones. Her hair was disheveled and there was a wild, hard exopthalamia where Candy's large but dewy eyes had been but moments before. The flesh around her mouth was taut, hard, sneering. Her body was tense as a striking cobra's, and her teeth—but this, I realize now, was a projection of my own instantaneous terror—seemed lined with blood, I mean sort of coated at the edges.

I was almost speechless. "In that case," I managed to say, instinctively guarding my loins with my left forearm, "who are you?"

"Wouldn't you like to know, Mr. Animal Headshrinker," said that unnatural, growling, animalistic voice. By this time the light in the bedroom had become nearly hallucinatory. Objects loomed. The skin on Candy's face seemed to mottle, first red, then blue, as if some shape were crawling around beneath it.

"Yes," I said decisively, not knowing what to expect but realizing that the simple happiness I had known until now with Candy was suddenly being shattered by something I did not understand. "I would like to know."

A hideous grin erupted on the strange creature's face. She cackled and then, unlike Candy ever would, she spat.

"Everything you like so much about Candy," I heard, as if from a million miles away, as air hammers began crunching away in my brain, "comes from me, Mildred. Her independence, her way with words, the way she wiggles that fanny of hers. That's all me, that simp couldn't get across the street by herself without old Mildred helping her."

I knew, and suspected, that I was about to enter a black hole from which I might never emerge, a hold so vast that even my conquering love for Candy might never, until the mystery were fully revealed, close.

That was Mildred's first visit. In the months that followed there have been hundreds of encounters with this strange, and as we know now artificial, personality, many of them bizarre—I mean the encounters—and all of them pointing to the U.S. Government as a machine of tyranny with no regard for human life.

-
-
-

"Candy?"

"Yes."

"Do you know where you are?"

"I'm in Langley, Virginia."

"And do you know who I am?"

"You're Bea Lin, the reclusive vegetable merchant of humble origins who rose to become the founder of an empire."

"But that's not really who I am, is it?"

"No, not really."

"What is it that I'm waving in front of your eyes?"

"A gold watch."

"And Candy Jones isn't really who you are, isn't that right?"

"That's right."

"Who are you really, Candy?"

"I'm Mildred. Mildred Huxley. I work for Bea Lin, the reclusive vegetable merchant and so on, just like Candy."

"But what Candy does for Bea Lin is a little different than what you do for Bea Lin, isn't that correct, Mildred?"

"I guess you hit the nail on the head, whoever you are."

"I'm your friend, Candy."

"I'm not Candy, I'm Mildred. I know you're my friend."

"Bea Lin wants you to go to China, Mildred."

"You're not Bea Lin."

"You're not Candy, either."

"You've got me there."

"Possibly. If you're discovered, Mildred, the best thing you can do is pretend to be Candy."

"They'd never fall for it. Candy is such a spineless nothing."

"A nonentity, we know this. Think of yourself as a method actress."

"I hate her. You don't know what it's like for me, sharing a body with that asshole. I mean, there's nobody home half the time. She can't even write a check for the gas bill without forgetting what she's doing after she gets the date filled in."

"But you're in control, Mildred. Candy is simply an implement."

"I guess you're right about that."

"I know I'm right, Mildred."

-
-
-

I can talk now.

It's all coming back to me. There, on the streets of Hong Kong. What I really can't believe is that I'm wearing that *dress*, Dick, you've never seen me in anything like *that*, I just wouldn't wear anything cut that way. I mean I look like some kind of lesbian from outer space in that dress. I just, I don't know, Dick, somehow I just don't think that's even me, I mean, I know they brainwashed me and everything but I cannot in a million years believe that even with my mind taken over I would be seen in something like that. The next image I get is that dry-cleaning establishment in

Kowloon, I was checked into the Hilton and I picked a guy up in the cocktail lounge and said I wanted to see some casinos. So I went over there with him on the boat, no, I didn't do it with him, give me a *break*, Dick, this was business, we already figured out all the times I had to put out for people on account of *business*, I really think you're being nasty when I'm honestly trying to get as much of this out as I can. Okay? So let's just drop the fucking angle, it didn't happen. I mean there I am with a blowgun full of curare getting ready to drop the blackjack dealer and you're worried about did I let some microchip salesman dick me for a half an hour or not, even if I did, you think I enjoyed it?

-
-

-

"We're here at 'Five Again All Night' and this is your good friend Ron, Ron Holloway, and I'm here with Candy Jones, the recently divorced wife of Dick Bridgely, world's foremost authority on animal neuroses, who claims that she was programmed by her husband to believe that she was brainwashed by the CIA and assumed a different identity as Mildred Huxley, possibly a professional assassin. You're on the beeper and we're ready for your questions."

"I'd like to know if your guest is acquainted with Silva Mind Control."

"Candy, would you care to comment?"

"Yes, I am acquainted with Silva Mind Control. But I believe the techniques which were used on me by my ex-husband were more advanced, for instance there are ways that the human mind can be given sudden commands across really extreme distances—"

"Would that be electrode implants you're referring to?"

"This is the mistake everybody makes when this subject comes up. What I am trying to explain, and in my book *The Ordeal of Candy Jones* I think I've made it clear, is that the government already controls everybody's mind. It's just when specific tasks come up that special techniques are used on individuals."

"Well, I'd have to agree with you on that. But what I'm curious about is how you discovered that it was your husband programming you instead of the CIA."

"It was both."

"Thanks for your call. Candy, would you elaborate on your last statement, that it was both?"

"My husband is employed by the CIA in animal experimentation. The CIA purchased his townhouse for him. Even if I didn't live a double life while I was working for Bea Lin Vegetables, and I'm still not sure, Dick himself did experiments on me for the government. First he implanted the idea that I had already been implanted with a second personality and had committed crimes all over the world, and then he tried to suggest, well, he succeeded I must say, he suggested that I may even have operated as a high-level call girl in order to kill a close associate of the former president of Nicaragua. Then he inspired me with guilt feelings which made me all the more eager to do whatever he asked me to do."

"And what specifically was that?"

"To kill Margaret Thatcher and Ronald Reagan."

"But you didn't do that."

"I should have, though. It would have rid me of guilt."

LEE EIFERMAN

Summer Flying

Waiting

She watched her mother measure the weeks by Thursday. On that
day the checks arrived in the mail, from her father. It was always
a handsome check, her mother claimed. And she watched her
mother dance around the room feigning sheer delight. "This check
is the biggest one ever. Don't you think so Marilyn?"
They were all about the same to her.
While watching the cars whizzing by her one after another, she
was reminded of her mother's Thursday. Her mother had grown
week by week away from her former husband's all-embracing love.
On Thursday her progress was confirmed.

Like the signing of a large sales deal, Marilyn noted. Or in this
situation, like a driver agreeing to offer me a ride.

A yellow pickup pulled over to the side of the road and gestured
for her to hop in. She left her broken car behind.

Blessings

Walter drove a van. A pickup van for the circus. He had all the
leisure-time gear in the back, he explained; a few cases of beer,
some fly-fishing reels, a game of chess and a TV.

What happened to your car? Walter asked.

Broken axle, it's rented. Marilyn was impatient to get to the airport. Waiting for a ride had exhausted her patience.

You from around these parts? Walter was. He also claimed he
knew a great place to eat lunch. She protested. She wasn't hungry.
He was.

And it was his car.

They stopped for some beer, peanuts, and slices of ham. Marilyn
was surprised to find herself in the situation she was in. She hadn't
taken a detour in years. Not since she left high school and decided
to skip college.

She asked Walter while they were still buying lunch what made
him stop.

You looked like you honestly were in trouble. It's fun being a hero.
Haven't you ever rescued anyone?

Walter's friendly intentions were clear.

You always travel alone?

He was interested in her stories. Where she had been, what she
sold for a living, and who she met on the way.

Time moved in lurches. They ate lunch on the side of a hill overlooking a raspberry patch. They picked dessert. Then they drank
some more beer. It was the most leisurely afternoon she had spent
since starting out on the road selling.

Marilyn was thinking about love and luck. Vaguely she wondered
who her next roommate would be, maybe she could afford living
alone. She thought about tomorrow, about her first board of directors meeting. She was filled with a warm glow. Finally she
simply watched a cloud go by.

Walter was no longer lying down. Nor was he looking at her. He
was looking at a bright orange bush. The bush, as he stood to

admire it, was moving slightly. Walter motioned to Marilyn to join him. With fingers pressed against his lips, he indicated that she should be silent.

She was lost. Transfixed by the sight of clouds rolling in, thicker and heavier. She felt free, even though the sky was becoming dense with dark clouds. She felt free. Released from obligations. In the dulling light of thickening clouds he could see the bush more clearly. When her attention snapped to the present, she became vaguely aware of Walter, this new person moving away from her without a word. She followed, impelled by a curiosity to follow his theatrically silent movements. Then she saw the bush in the distance. It seemed to gleam, emanating its own light.

Like Moses seeing the burning bush, Walter whispered.

They walked downhill toward it. As they got closer, Walter and Marilyn slowed down in unison. The shrub was covered with bright orange monarch butterflies. The butterflies alighted, drawn there by the bright neon orange of these flowers. A perfect camouflage.

They stopped. The butterflies, upset by a strange presence, froze in their sucking action and took flight. Marilyn and Walter stood still.

And then the butterflies circled around them in clockwise lilting movements. Gently up and down they danced around Walter and around Marilyn. The dance lasted a few moments. A dance without the rhythm of inhale and exhale. Enough to complete a petal's breath of circling. The butterflies landed on the flowers.

Again, Marilyn was aware of the present moment.

Nearby there was a pond and Marilyn with Walter's prodding peeled off her hot sticky shirt and went swimming. Just before it rained they both plunged in.

When they emerged it was pouring and lightning had split the dark bank of clouds twice. Shifting higher in the sky, the lightning struck a third time closer to the center of the storm.

Near where they stood. They ran then, seeing the lightning hit overhead. They ran in unison.

Power

Walter dropped her off at the airport that same afternoon. At 4
P.M. sharp she caught a small plane going from Dallas to Houston.
Walter didn't linger. She was expected to attend a board of directors meeting the next morning at 9 A.M. Still the image of the
butterflies, the sense of light wings brushing her arms softly made
her pause in her adjustments. Ordinarily an automatic response
to plane travel, her hand hesitated while adjusting the seat belt.

Other thoughts, other strategies needed her attention. Savoring
the flavor of the berries, or searching for little hard seeds nestled
in her teeth was the backdrop for studying her statistics. She was
determined to succeed and impress upon the Board her worth.
She carried her neat pile in her suitcase.

After the plane took off, she pulled out the slim folder containing
these figures. The presentation was impressive. The colors chosen
by the art department depicting regional sales were on the mark,
hushed tones of maroon and salmon pink. Downbeat.

Conveying a sense of sloping profits in other regions. Was she
blessed with good salesmanship, or was it the wealth of her as-
signed area?

She wanted to make her competitor, Bill, explain the drop in sales.
It wasn't specifically Bill's responsibility, but it was a convenient
place to lay blame.

As the plane began its descent she was too distracted to notice
the wheels failing to engage. She was planning how one might
shift power bases.

Adventure

When Marilyn looked around her, the passengers were spilling
into the aisles. The stewardess could barely be seen in the left
corner of the cabin struggling to get to the microphone. And the
plane, which Marilyn vaguely remembered descending for a landing was now heading up again. It was a small plane with room for

about twelve passengers. And all twelve faces, white with terror, were pressing toward the aisles. Her mind leaped from statistics to her shoes. If the plane was forced to crash land, her beautiful soft brown suede heels would be cumbersome in a burning wreck. While the plane ascended and the captain spoke calmly to the passengers about their current emergency, Marilyn changed into her sneakers. The stewardess, finally in possession of her microphone, was explaining how a parachute works.

Marilyn tied her shoelaces. This is a rip cord.

Marilyn realized she would have to leave behind the slim folder, as well as her suitcase and new attaché case. All the evidence of her latest success.

When you land keep your knees bent. It's a beautiful experience, go with it, the stewardess advised.

In the rush of the moment, Marilyn eyed her shoulder bag with pleasure. A short blonde woman, evidently an executive as well, was trying to stuff her wallet and key ring into a small skirt pocket. With sneakers and handbag Marilyn bravely stepped forward. At the newly opened plane door, the stewardess was surrounded by a band of anxious passengers. A young man in his early thirties was eager to get out of the plane before it crashed. He demanded a parachute. The plane was running low on fuel. The captain calmly informed the passengers: Soon we will be attempting a crash landing. A mother had a child in her arms and was trying to convince the captain of the wisdom of landing in the field below. The captain insisted above the din of the weakening engine that he was going to attempt a landing in the next field, over the ridge. It's flatter, much safer.

The tightening fist of passengers parted and allowed the young man with his parachute to head toward the open plane door.

Marilyn was standing so close to him that she felt that she easily could have jumped out with him. Someone stopped her.

The stewardess handed her a parachute and instructed her when to pull the cord. There was an awesome silence of whistling air, and a great yawning height below her. She sat down at the edge of the plane, imitating the young man as he prepared to leap out. The other passengers, a vague presence behind her, pushed themselves closely around her to get a sense of the edge. The stewardess said something to her which Marilyn couldn't hear. A pair of goggles were handed to her. Marilyn had to let go of the door handle in order to adjust the fit of the goggles. At that moment, with her legs dangling over the edge and arms stretched over her head, Marilyn felt light, free and eager to jump. The goggles were in place. She jumped.

Love

It was so easy. Gliding in the air with the wind whistling through your teeth. With goggles on. Soaring with arms spread out. Able to see wide distances. Like an eagle. And then at the same time falling. Falling into soft mother earth. Soft cushioning mother earth. Marilyn landed in a hay field. She felt blessed. Standing up with the wind whistling in her ears, her breath returned to her. In short spurts. Over the hay field she crawled, not daring to stand again on her shaky knees.

Finally breathing almost normally, she tried standing. In the road across the field a woman was standing on the roof of her car, straining to see. Marilyn waved and waved again. The woman drew her binoculars to her eyes. Toward the hay stack. Where Marilyn was. Marilyn stood still. She hoped the woman would spot her. Maybe she watched me fall from the sky.

While the woman studied her, Marilyn noticed the plane explode into a bright orange ball and career across the sky, over the ridge. Just as the pilot had insisted.

The woman climbed off the roof of the car, and motioned Marilyn to join her.

A few miles down the road, they spotted the burning plane. Marilyn thought of her attaché case, her blue woolen suit and makeup collection all burning in the wreckage. There was a strange overpowering smell that became stronger the closer they came. The scene of the wreckage seemed unreal. As if it belonged to a film. It didn't seem to be in the province of real life. A TV crew, someone whispered, was on its way. It was a relief to hear that. It would be documented.

When the police finally arrived, they announced that all survivors of the wreckage must report to the town hospital. The ambulances however had not yet arrived. It's required, warned the spectators, who had no claim on the incident, before you can collect on insurance. It's down Route 45.

Luckily for Marilyn the woman volunteered to drive her to town. It's really not very far, the woman reassured her.

In the car, Marilyn confessed to feeling fine. No broken bones. She was sure. Nothing hurt. She gently poked at herself just to be certain.

Brandy? You could probably use some. The woman, introducing herself as Sarah, kept some in her glove compartment for emergencies. It was a small bottle of cognac. Sarah directed the car over to the side of the road. To collect herself, she explained. Marilyn was thinking about parachuting. She was remembering the freedom of flight.

What an experience! Sarah was now drinking the cognac as well. She seemed envious. Marilyn, despite the cognac, was squirming under Sarah's scrutiny.

Marilyn turned the conversation round.

Do you live around here? It occurred to Marilyn that it was the second time in one day she had asked this question. Am I becoming a hitchhiker?

Sarah was not a native to this area. But yes, she had lived around the area. She owned a restaurant. A Mexican restaurant.

You don't look Mexican.

Sarah's family were from Poland and Yugoslavia. They came to the States in the 50s illegally.

My parents were real mavericks. Sarah was evidently proud of herself. They drove slowly to the hospital. It's small, Sarah explained, as if she were preparing Marilyn for the ordeal that lay ahead. Twelve injured people will cause a riot in that emergency room. They skipped the hospital.

Maybe another day you could go there, when it's less busy.

Sarah suggested an alternate destination. Her restaurant. When they arrived Sarah ordered them dinner. And then they relaxed.

Concerning the Future

When she woke up the next morning, Marilyn found out where she was. From an ashtray on her bed. It read: Greetings from Dime Box Texas.

There was a faint taste of cognac in her mouth, and a trail of Mexican spices. The air smelled moist, sweet. Maybe there was a lake nearby. Sarah was gone. Her side of the bed was empty.

There was a note tacked to the bedroom mirror saying, See ya in awhile. Today we go swimming. Marilyn had to keep her professional urgency at bay. A board of directors meeting would be taking place momentarily. Only at that moment, the moment when she was reading the bedroom note and smelling the sweet moisture in the air, did she realize that she had lost her watch as well.

Every attempt at orientation defied her. Time had disappeared. Or transformed hours into rough estimations. How long had it been since I knew the time? Since meeting Walter?

She should have called her office. Or at the very least the police. She probably would be listed among the dead or presumed dead. An irresponsible delight shuttled through her. A chill of anticipation. A northerner settling down in Texas. Oil and scrubbed-clean, sun-bleached terrain. Sounds of revving engines, of trucks and big souped-up vans. Hot Mexican chili. Thoughts that go straight as arrows.

Swimming at the lake in the afternoon, Marilyn again toyed with the idea of calling the office. A young man at that moment, at that intersection between thought and action, scooped her up in his arms and laughingly tossed her off the boat dock. Into the water. When she surfaced a handsome crowd of men and women had gathered at the boat dock. They were laughing and watching Marilyn bubble up for air. Their bodies were firm and tanned.

Sarah was there as well. In a stark white bathing suit and a blonde in her arms, Sarah was beckoning Marilyn out of the water.

The sun caught the glint of wetness condensing on a bottle of beer as it was posed high in the air. Marilyn slipped out of the water. The young men and women formed a thick circle around her.

Each face was eager and open. Waiting to discover who she was. Dripping wet on the dock, Marilyn sipped her beer and watched the sun setting behind a distant hill. She looked at the lake and soft folds of land surrounding it. She knew it would be very easy land to sell. The prospect was exciting.

REINALDO POVOD

Things to Do Today

Don't tell, okay? . . . alright? . . . Promise . . .
Cross your heart & hope to die . . . Yeah, do it . . .
Now get away from me.

One thing I gotta do is, I gotta send Papi a birthday card. Boy, it's too bad I can't send'im a present . . . But, I ain't got no money . . . Besides, they don't allow gifts of any kind over there at Danbury Prison . . . I can't wait till he gets out.

Please, God, do me a favor . . . Don't let Papi find out about, what . . . you know . . . I did! Please . . . Boy, you know, I wish I knew why God is letting certain things happen to me. Hey, you know, I'm only thirteen. Give me a break . . . Dios apreta, pero no ahoga, like Abuelita always says. God tightens his grip, but he doesn't strangle us . . . I hope Granny is right.

You see, in January, Abuelita—Granny—was checking Cookie's Fruit of the Looms, & boy did I perspire. You see, Cookie, is this ten year ol' boy Granny promised to take care of . . . for a fee, of course. And if she knew what he & me did . . . boy she'd . . . I don't know what . . . You know, if she'd put a boiled egg in my mouth for cussing, I can't imagine what she would do to me—for what I did to Cookie. But I didn't do nothin' . . . Really, I didn't.

Anyway . . . She's really getting into inspecting Cookie's underwears . . . She brings 'em up to the light, runs her fingers thru the seams . . . What is she looking for? . . . Bloodstains? Nah, only girls have that problem . . . Anyway, whatever it is that she is looking for, she's not giving up until she finds it . . . Not satisfied with one pair, she digs into the dirty laundry bag, looking for another pair of his stinky underwears . . . & another & another & another—until . . . Finally she finds what she had suspected . . . Ronnie?! . . . On one of MY stinky-smelly underwears! . . . WHAT? . . . I mean, que Granny? . . . What's this? . . . That? . . . this . . . Ahhh . . . Ahhhh nothin', tan mucho cuidado, you better be careful . . . It ain't nothin', Granny . . . Oh, no? . . . it looks like somethin' to me . . . That, o' that's just snot . . . Oh, yeah? . . . ye-yes, I ah, used it to blow my nose, you know, Granny? . . . She didn't say nothing, she knew I was lying, she knew what it was . . . it was semen.

I swear, I still didn't do nothing . . . I was simply sitting on the sofa, watching T.V., minding my own business, when HE comes over, Cookie, yeah-yes, & sits, blop, right on my lap . . . I know, I should of push'd him off, but . . . I didn't . . . He's a cute kid, I thought . . . What the . . . it's a cute thing . . . You know, to wanna come over & wanna be buddies . . . Boy, was I wrong . . . He starts to wiggle his little behind, & I . . . you know, start to get hard, very hard—it inflated like a raft . . . HOLY COW, as Phil Rizzuto says: WATTA HARD-ON! I grab'd him & putta vice grip hold on'im & kissed the back of his lil' head. Oh, I say, 'bout . . . two dozen time . . . I tell'ya, I closed my eyes, & I was in Love . . . I was doing exactly like the guy & the girl does on T.V. Harold? . . . Yes, my love? . . . Harold, kiss me, you fucker! . . . I lower'd my pants, drop'd 'em like an egg, but I didn't take off my underwears, I stay'd in my undies . . . I didn't even lower his pants . . . I only, you know, wiggled. Boy, did we wiggle—sparks flew outta his lil' culito. Cookie shook his moneymaker so hard, that . . . that was, why I . . . I stained my undies.

Things I've Done Today

I, ah, read . . . I really dug this line I read in one of those pamphlets the Jesus Freaks hand out to people . . . I was, ya know, walking around & ah . . . it was between taking a free pack of sample cigarettes on this corner—oh, yeah, by the way, dig this: the free cigarettes were being handed out right next to a blood pressure stand that was also set up on the corner. Only in the city so nice that they had to name it twice could this happen! I took the pamphlet.

Here's the line: Remove the rationalization & you will find peace of mind. I'm gonna try doing just that.

Things I Won't Do Today

I won't stay away from Cookie . . . I ain't gonna push 'im away anymore. Let's see what happens.

Things I've Done Today

I was in my room laying on my bed watching T.V. when Cookie comes over & sits in this chair I got next to the T.V. set, facing me, which makes it very difficult for the person in this chair to watch the T.V. The only way is to put yer face right up to the glass, or . . . if I invite ya to sit on my bed.

Hey . . . yeah? . . . You wanna watch T.V.? . . . Yeah . . . C'mere, sit over here . . . There? . . . Yeah, next to me . . . He was kind of puzzled 'cause I usually throw 'im off the bed & lately he's been sitting in that chair . . . He comes over & I thought: When this guy grows up he's gonna be gettin' more ass than a toilet seat, 'cause he's such a good-looking guy. Better lookin' than me, almost!

He lays down next to me . . . that was cool . . . though I told him to sit, it seemed harmless . . . At ten years ol' they're into, Monkey see, Monkey do . . . We thirteen year ol' guys know all about that.

So, you know, I ignore it & I try to get in some serious cartoon action when outta the corner of my eye I notice that when I cross my legs, he crosses his. I fold my arms, the little monkey would fold his & I try to ignore this too . . . But I couldn't, ya see, 'cause I got a habit of stickin' my hands down into my drawers & you know kind'a playin' around wit the family jewels.

Hey? . . . Wha? . . . Whatta ya' doin? . . . Huh? . . . Playing wit yer pee-pee? He starts to giggle & he says to me: Are you? I say to 'im, No . . . Oh yeah . . . Git yer hands outta there . . . No . . . Why not? . . . 'Cause . . . 'Cause nothin', just get yer fuckin' hands outta there!

He don't say nothin', he just stares back at me, looking scared. I . . . you know, then reach over to pull his hands out & he turns on his side, you know, giving me his back & I, you know, I gotta reach way over. When I do he starts to struggle & giggle & I begin to wrestle wit 'im, until . . . he ends up on top of me . . . Yeah, I know, but I don't know what happened . . . Real passionate shit though . . . You know what I didn't expect?

Was . . . that I somehow—man, I dug what was happening to me . . . And I knew what I was doin' . . . You wanna know how I knew?

—When I was young, I mean, real young . . . my father came home early one day & found my brother & me in our undies, playing on the floor wit our G.I. Joe's . . .

Who left yous alone? he says. He sounded real pissed off.

Mami, I say,

Git over there, he says to me . . . I flew.

Get in there, you . . . he says to my brother, givin 'im a whack on the back of the head to get him started.

I didn't do nothin' . . . my brother was saying as my ol' man slammed the bedroom door . . . Please, Pop, don't hit me, my brother kept whining. Please don't hit me! WHAT THE FUCK WERE YOU TWO DOING? . . . HUH?!

Playing . . .

PLAYING?!!

Yeah.

Don't lie to me . . . DON'T LIE TO ME.

I swear, Pop . . . please.

IN YER UNDERWEARS?!! WHATSA MATTER, YER GOT NO FREAKIN' PANTS. HUH?

Yeah.

HUH?

YES, YES. YES. Please, Pop.

Suddenly the door opened. Git in here!

I went in, & I saw my brother sobbing on the floor.

Git up on that chair.

Please, Pop, don't hit me . . . I pleaded.

SHUT THE FUCK UP!

And he yanked my undies all the way down to my ankles.

Grab the back of the chair.

Huh?

THIS! THIS!! . . . & he slammed the back of the chair I was standing on for emphasis.

I did & felt a breeze shoot up my ass.

Then I felt my father's thumbs spread my cheeks.

Ugh!

Felt his hot breath on my ass & that sent a shiver up my spine.

Put yer underwears back on . . . he growled . . . then left the room to wash his hands . . . I quickly pulled those suckers up, then I sat on the chair waiting for him to come back & say it was alright to go back & play . . .

He never did.

& he made me feel I was doing something very wrong.

Like I now know what I'm doing is just as bad . . .

But never worse than to have been accused of . . . yeah, fucking wit yer brother.

I hold Cookie . . . tight, you know, try to squeeze the living shit outta 'im. Think about maybe trying to do something else to 'im, but um . . . But nah, man . . . you know I think about my father & ah . . . I love 'im, wanna be like 'im . . . Huh? Cookie says, looking at me. Nothing, I say to 'im. I get this image of my father's face, the same kind of expression he had when he went to jail, he was like gonna cry, & this brings me back & I feel like the father & Cookie's the son & . . . we just fall asleep.

I don't know if Cookie brought the man out in me, or . . . if I brought out the woman in him . . .

Either way, I . . . I know I'm a man . . . 'Cause ya see when me & him were together . . . I held him, he didn't hold me . . . Just like when I use to sleep wit Papi . . . He, ah, you know, use to sleep sideways wit one arm under my head & the other arm around my waist . . . the same way he slep wit moms, so ya see . . . I'm the man & remember, it was Cookie who sat up on my lap, not me on his . . . just like I use to do with my Pops . . . Pop never sat on my lap, right? . . . Right. & to prove it, when Cookie woke up, he still wanted to play & I had this boner . . . He ast me if he could see it. I said t' him if he don't quit botherin' me & leave me alone I was gonna put it in his mouth.

Go 'head, he said.

I coulda, you know, said to him, lemme see yours first, if I really liked boys ya know?

But I ain't into that, I don't wanna see his . . . see it.

I don't like boys!

Stop, I say t' him.

He just giggles, & grabs it.

I coulda, ya know, gotten right up & gone into the living room where Granny—Abuelita—was rappin' on the phone.

But I get mad, & I say t' him, look!

I show 'im my thing.

Stop, I'm warning you, stoppit.

He licked it.

Licked it like a Popsicle.

His tongue felt warm, hot . . . & as soft as the time I licked Mami's tit-tee.

'Cept hers felt like jello.

See, I was 'bout . . . his age . . . Foolin' around, I was copying how a dog walks & wags his tail. I was on all fours, raisin' hell, when you know, my mother goes to smack me & when she does I spring up at her & tear her blouse. Then . . . I don't give her no time to cover herself with her hands & I JUMP UP . . . & lick her tit-tees . . .

Making that strange sound, you know that begging sound dogs make when they know they've been bad on the floor.

She swung from her ankles and . . . smacked me like a dog.

Bad boy, bad boy.

Hate his 'lil freakin' ass for what happened, ya know? . . . though, I . . . never actually done anything' to 'im. The thing is . . . Bro, I never ever gotten that close to someone 'cept my father & when my mother comes around t' see me I kiss 'er, or . . . when I leave to go out ta the street, I always kiss my grandmother & I ask 'er for her blessing: Benedicion, 'buelita . . . you know? . . . I don't know.

JOAN HARVEY
Plagiarism

It is my job to keep the house clean. There is little furniture, so it is mostly a job of scrubbing, washing and waxing the tiles, removing hairs from the drain in the sink. The house is quite large. I have my own room at the top of the stairs.

I have received a letter from my father's lawyer telling me of all the money my father has given me that I am not allowed to spend. I paint the walls of my room white, except for one, and that I paint the color of Rome.

The fat man comes in. *"Je n'écoute que pour le plaisir de redire,"* he says.

"Diderot," I reply.

"I have nothing to say for myself," he says. "Nothing. And now lunch is being served."

My father turned me over to the fat man at the earliest opportunity. It was a deal they made. But I don't mind. My father is a real bastard and the fat man only has his habits.

———

We eat in a room that is bright and yellow. The food is spread like a picnic on the floor. The fat man eases himself down beside me. "Leila," he says. "You've been jumping over the fire again. The bottoms of your trousers are scorched."

The whole house is wired with hidden microphones and cameras. The fat man likes to watch things from the comfort of his bed. The walls of his room are draped with a soft, rose-colored fabric and the floor is piled high with chicken bones he has sucked meat from in the night.

On the wall of the fat man's room is a photograph of a young man lying seductively on a divan with a veil covering his eyes. The man holds a pear in one hand and his penis pokes gently out of the white sheets that hide his lower body. The divan is covered with chicken grease, or possibly ink or blood. The young man is my lover.

I go out at night to a rocky place where we build the fire. My friends come too and we chase each other and leap over the flames again and again until we are scorched and glowing with heat. Then we return to the house and bathe and make love and eat as the fat man watches from his bed.

My lover has no money and gives the impression of being somewhat helpless. He likes to examine the Greek vases and tiny sculptures that I stole from his father. He makes plans for our future.

"Eventually," he says, "we will have children we feel ill-equipped to deal with. We will keep strong fronts."

We desire each other intensely.

All day I scrub, working my sponge over the lemon-colored tiles in the dining room, the sky-blue tiles in the kitchen, the rose-colored tiles in the fat man's bedroom. My back grows sore as I water the stately palm trees that are the main ornaments in the house. Visitors pass in and out on their way to see the fat man who is an important person here. It's because he is a dealer. Although he says it's because he sleeps alone.

My lover takes me out to dinner and lets me pay the bills. Because he has no money he thinks I should make a marriage of convenience. He has important plans for me. "There are plenty of men in this world," he says. "No reason why you can't get a good one." At the next table five Japanese men sit in a semicircle around a tall ravishing blonde.

"Let your imagination run wild," my lover says.

But then he tells me not to stare too much.

When the fat man is lonely, as he sometimes is, he comes to my room and sits on a chair by the bed. He strokes the tiny asthmatic dog he keeps with him, and he looks at me with his large selfish eyes.

"Existing is plagiarism," he says.

"Cioran," I answer.

He asks me to beat him, but I refuse.

"Imagine," he says, "my bare buttocks quivering across your lap."

I laugh. He does not realize the kind of beating I would give him if I had the chance.

The visitors believe that I, too, have a certain kind of power because I am allowed to live in the fat man's house. They do favors for me, in hope that I will help them to get on his good side. I don't tell them that the fat man's ways are fixed, completely, so that I cannot influence him in any way. Occasionally my father comes to visit and the fat man lets me watch on the TV monitors as he makes my father squirm.

My lover wants to take me away to live with him, but I tell him I don't like furniture. "I've been thinking it's time you got a new lover," the fat man says. I agree. He gets out his collection of photographs and lets me have a look. I wonder how each picture will look hanging above his bed. Finally I choose a man who is wearing round dark glasses so I can barely make out his eyes. He is wearing a small black pair of bathing trunks, white sneakers and white socks. He is sitting with one foot raised aggressively in the air. There is a toothpick protruding at an angle from between his teeth.

"Good," the fat man says. "I'll see what I can do."

The moments when I hang in the air over the fire are the moments when I am most who I am.

"You've got bad habits," the fat man says. He is looking at my scorched feet.

"What about you?" I ask. He's been shooting up whenever he gets the chance. He lies on the bed and watches a video called "Overdose." He likes the feeling of the needles in his skin.

My lover no longer comes around. The fat man made a deal. Every now and then he stops by my room and I see the needle tracks running up and down his arm.

"Imitation is criticism," he says.

"Blake," I say. "You're slipping."

I clean the rooms one by one, yellow, blue, rose. The fat man is lying on his face by the side of his bed, a needle hanging from his arm. I clear the chicken bones from around the bed and take the little dog in my arms. I know it is up to me now. I move my belongings into his room and continue the business myself. I have all the contacts.

The man with the round dark glasses has come to stay in my old room. He does the cleaning now and I let him go out at night. At lunchtime he joins me in the room with the lemon-colored tiles.

"*Je n'écoute que pour le plaisir de redire,*" I say.

"What?" he says. He has a lot to learn.

"Later I'll show you some photographs," I say. I look down and notice that the bottoms of his trousers are very slightly burned.

DON SKILES

The Loft

Henschel over again today. Stove did not work right; both of us
at it for an hour; flue plugged up. Room full of smoke which H
complained of . . . We sat there in our overcoats, drinking tea with
mittens on; recalled grade school days. H says cold intolerable;
asks why more places don't have fireplaces. Talking about fireplaces in San Francisco, in the East, in England. Henschel told
me about a party where a fireplace didn't work, and the firemen
came in the middle of the party. H says somebody ought to write
a book on fireplaces.

Both of us coughing, cursing. Why do we live like this? he says.

Car out of commission. Battery dead. Run down by defective al-
ternator. Eats money like gas. Received phone call; Carlson in
hospital with ailment again; a bad business.

Went to see Carlson at horsepistol; late in leaving here, so arrived
past visiting hours. Guard would not allow me in, argument en-
sued—threat of arrest, pushing match. Other guards came. Thrown
out. Streets full of glacial slush, frozen sharp. Fucking endless

misery of winter. Got back, fell asleep in stupor; woke and thought the room was upside down; it slowly righted itself.

Henschel over. Pulls up pants leg to show his long johns. "What a place!" he says. "You have to go around wearing thermal underwear—like fucking Antarctica." He speaks about the great and awful winter five years ago; stabs a finger—"*You* were in California, like a commercial." We laughed then . . . Looking out the window; saw cold blackness of winter night; terrible. The window grimy, industrial, warehouse vintage. Can imagine a crystal clear clean one, glass so clean it squeaks. Henschel suddenly recalls the phrase "Bet she'd give you a boner." Standing there, with a lonely adolescent hard-on, pledging allegiance to the flag. School.

Henschel shows up with Vic Cozzoli, guy who works in a bakery, a photographer. The bakery sounds like a factory from his description of it. He's able to take a good deal of stuff from the place, though; good stuff to eat . . . Vic talked for several hours about "places to go;" we drank all the vodka I had. Cozzoli thought the following places would be "neat" to go to:

Bicycle through South and North Dakota
Banff, Canada
Prince Edward Island, Canada and New Brunswick, Canada
Ashville, North Carolina
Cape Hatteras, North Carolina
Nantucket
Montreal
Toronto—the "Rome" of North America
Savannah, Georgia
Charleston, South Carolina

The man who walks the floor, in the other loft. Country 'n' western music played by a Chinese woman disc jockey named Mimi. Told Henschel all night dj would be good job . . . "Your local dj . . ."

The light from the skylight, at a certain hour, moves up the white wall so fast it is like a burning.

Heard people screwing in the next loft; laid there and listened to it. Hollow. Can't be too many things worse than having to lay there and listen to that.

Tonight, let it be Lowenbrau.

H says must control Scorpio side. Must regularly review chart, aspects, balancing. Cusp person. H shows me gold Cross pen; tells me these impress executives these days. H grins; says, "*Rolling Stone* takes these things seriously." Asked Henschel how he knew all this stuff. "It's my business to know these things," he says.

Read in paper that the supposed body of a murdered man, shipped to his family, was someone else.

Brunner, Henschel, Cozzoli and myself at Henschel's. Studio so cold/damp Henschel fears arthritis, rheumatism, chilblains, nephritis; says he wants to move to San Diego. "Down in Dago, man! Seventy, eighty degrees all the time! Very sweet. Next to Mexico, too. No fog, no damp, no winter. Think of it."

"The sun shines all the time. It never rains. Gets boring," Brunner said, shrugging.

Vic says he went to dentist; smelled food cooking as dentist drilled; inquired with eye motions, grunts.

"Beef teriyaki," the dentist said.

Henschel depressed that his girl is also going with another man. "She's blowing him so much she's getting a moustache!" he said bitterly.

Brunner says he falls in love constantly, a hundred times a day, in the streets, on the bus, on the subways, in restaurants, over the telephone, going through stores, in elevators, passing cars. Wonders how anyone can get married, be faithful, stay in love. His latest girlfriend (he calls them his "ladies") is in a New Wave band called Permanent Wave. They played a bill at the Elite Club with Pressing Issues, and the Zero Boys.

Drank all of Henschel's booze; left in early a.m. ice streets. Brunner commented on the neon lights on the ice. Desperate feeling of loneliness.

While we walked up the alley behind H's studio, a bomb went off in a building downtown. Sirens wailing. Did not know what to make of this. Vic said a refinery blew up several days ago; berated me for not watching tv.

Talked about the "even keel"—the illusion fed us that we must "get our lives on an even keel!" Cozzoli laughed, and said, "Sure. America's a country where you have to go into the hospital to get a rest."

Saw a license plate go by that read MS MORR. Brunner walks with head down, says, "Fucking shit . . . "

Still snowing after four-day storm of it. Sat in hot tub for *frisson*; drank hot tea. Too much salicylate in tea, though . . . Received letter from Jere Montag, out of nowhere. Now living on a farm, in a barn, in upstate New York. Thirty below zero, and cross country skiing. In good shape. Cannot figure out why he's there, except for the woman he mentions; says she is "like 50's motel furniture—blond and tacky." Says there are Mexicans, farm laborers, stranded up there after late harvest season. Strange. Near a place called Warsaw, New York, where he says washing machines are made; only local industry.

Had temp job downtown. Hid out in the john in the afternoon. Made observances—as Brunner recommends, "Never let them force you to waste any time." By two o'clock, after lunch, you can see the shined shoes of each guy on either side of your stall. The shitter is going full-blast; snorts, grunts, sighs, ripper farts, thundering blow-outs, all simultaneously; one guy leaves, another takes his place very shortly. All look neat and natty outside in the hall. They make large, significant decisions in their glassed-in offices. An audio tape alone of this would change corporate image . . .

unbelievable work they gave me to do; could make nothing of it. Fear, sweating.

Bath house across the street burned down in middle of night. Woken in night first by screams. Saw two guys pull two women out of their car, beat them; neighbor downstairs called cops. "What did we do? What did we do?" I could hear one woman saying . . . Police and firemen arrive almost together; garish lights, smoke, steam, boomed voices on intercoms, radio static. No sleep. Had been up late calling high school reunion; thought it interesting to do. Talked to guy who used to live up the street from me, and I could see his face, as it was then. Now works with computers; says he comes through here sometimes, and will call. Had suddenly no sense of time, on phone.

Henschel says the liberation of cottage industries is "right around the corner."

At temp job, a man went out of it, and began playing strange tapes hidden in his desk. They gave him a leave, they said . . . came home, and got notice of rent increase; also new building manager— have to keep an eye on that.

Someone wrote "POEMS," with an arrow pointing up the street, on the sidewalk.

Sent Brunner and Henschel a note, in which I said, "Everything is coming together; I'm coming apart."

Find that I ramble in my thoughts increasingly to remembrances of boyhood; fishing in creeks and the river on summer mornings, with the light mist lifting off; green screens of trees. Walking in the streets, thinking this! Is everyone walking around like this? . . . What is everyone thinking of in the street? If you could go up to a random number, in just a few blocks, and ask them— would they tell you? What would they say?

Hassles with the plumbing. Air hammer pipes, among other things. Hassles with food storage, and with locks on the outside door. Jesus. Saw photo of "Your Home" in a magazine; long, cheery, yellow house, in leafy trees, with white trimmed shutters.

Pulled a filling out eating a piece of candy Vic left. I called him, and he asked me to think of how many ground-up cows I'd eaten in my life.

Everyone's wearing bomber jackets. This must be the Year of the Bomber Jacket. Last year it was Racing Stripe Jackets. But the really in jacket is "distressed leather," to be worn with a pair of very faded out, nearly white, jeans . . .

Need to get some earplugs.

Graffiti increasing, especially on the buses:

Eat The Dead
Motorhead
Air Head Tex—'81
Hollywood Pimps
On Acid
Ingrid is a fat, sleazy cow who devirginated herself with a hot dog
Suck
US Out of El Salvador! Victory to Leftist Insurgents!

Brunner wonders if he should go to a therapist.

Can't seem to keep the place clean, although try to. Seems defeating. Desire to whitewash whole place. Locks on door make it look like the Bastille; women afraid to come up. Abstinence record of two and a half months, or so.

Henschel and Brunner over. Henschel says the stock market is about to rise, as it did in 1929, after the crash, and that now is the time to invest. Brunner ill with earache; told of quote from art magazine: "The rich are still rich, the poor poor, but everyone is an artist."

Henschel says if one could set a goal to be well-off in 8 or 10 years, it could be achieved. Then one could "kick back," as he likes to say, and "enjoy life . . . kick back by the pool, you know."

Brunner said success was probably like a blanket, and that painting was really about having beers with your friends. Recommended eating fresh mangoes, bananas and fish. Told him that I'd never been able to take things seriously; he said, "Neither have I, but I act as if I do. You have to learn to do that—people take you to be mature, then."

Vic called; had little to say. "Just calling," he said. Did say that Henschel told him that he had his ass pinched on an elevator by a woman.

Wrote down the names of the members of my family, and looked at them; those names. Wrote them down again. Have written them down at night many times, to remind me to write a letter to them, etc. All back in that small town . . . when I said that I wondered what those people do, Vic said, "They eat the world's shit—that's what they do."

Need to get a new journal. Like the ones now from China, mainland China, with exotic, colored covers. Nice.

Read that Jefferson dined alone in the White House.

Today, in the street, I saw a man reach up as he passed and touch the branches of a tree.

LYNNE TILLMAN

Dead Talk

I am Marilyn Monroe and I'm speaking from the dead. Actually I left a story behind. I used to be jealous of people who could write stories, and maybe that's why I fell in love with a writer, but that doesn't explain Joe. Joe had other talents. I didn't even know how famous he was when we met. Maybe I was the only person in America who didn't. I was glad he was famous, it made it easier for a while, and then it didn't matter, even though we fit together that way. The way men and women sometimes fit together. It doesn't last. I got tired of watching television. Sex is important but like anything that's important, it dies or causes trouble. Arthur didn't watch television, he watched me. People thought of us like a punchline to a dirty joke. Or maybe we had no punchline, I don't know. Anything I did was a double entendre. It was different at the beginning, beginnings are always different.

Before I was Marilyn Monroe, I felt something shaking inside me, Norma Jean. I guess I knew something was going to happen, that I was going to be discovered. I was all fluttery inside, soft. I was working in a factory when the first photographs were taken. It was during the war and my husband was always fighting. I was alone for the first time in my life. But it was a good alone, not a bad alone. Not like it got later. I was about to start my life, like pressing my foot on the gas pedal and just saying GO. And the photographs, the first photographs, showed I could get that soft look on my face. That softness was right inside me and I could call it up. Everything in me went up to the surface, to my skin, and the glow that the camera loved, that was me. I was burning up inside.

Marilyn put her diary on the night table and knocked over many bottles of pills. Some were empty, so that when they hit the white carpeted floor they didn't make a sound. Marilyn made a sound for them, something like whoosh or oops, and as she bent over she pulled her red silk bathrobe around her, covering her breasts incompletely so that she could look down at them with a mixture of concern and fascination. Her body was a source of drama to her, almost like a play, with its lines and shapes and meanings that it gave off. And this was something, she liked to tell her psychiatrist, that just happened, over which she had had no control. After three cups of coffee the heaviness left her body. The day was bright and cloudless and nearly over. She thought about how the sky looked in New York City, filled with buildings, and how that was less lonely to look at.

Marilyn just wanted to be loved. To be married forever and to have babies like every other woman. Her body, in its dramatic way, had other ideas. Her vagina was too soft, a gynecologist once told her, and Marilyn imagined that was a compliment, as if she were a good woman because her vaginal walls hadn't gotten hard. Hard and mean. But maybe that's why she couldn't keep a baby, her uterus just wouldn't hold one, wouldn't be the strong walls the baby needed. Marilyn's coffee cup was next to her hand mirror and she was lying on her white bed looking up at the mirrored ceiling. She was naked now, which was the way she liked to be all the time. When she was a child, the legend goes, she wanted to take off all her clothes in church, because she wanted to be naked in front of God. She wanted him to adore her by her adoring him through her nakedness. To Marilyn love and adoration were the same.

Marilyn took the hand mirror and opened her legs. Her pubic hair was light brown and matted, a real contrast to the almost white hair on her head, which had been done the day before. It was as if they were parts of two different bodies, one public, one private. My pubic hair is Norma Jean, how I was born, she once wrote in her diary. It was hot and the air conditioner was broken. She could smell her own smell, which gave atmosphere to the drama. Her legs were open as wide as they could go and Marilyn placed the mirror at her cunt and studied it, the opening into her. Sometimes she thought of it as her ugly face, sometimes as a funny face. She made it move by flexing the muscles of her vagina.

He said he'd marry me but now I know he was lying. He said I should understand his position and have some patience. After all he has children and a wife. I told him I could wait forever if he just gave me some hope.

Marilyn took the hand mirror and held it in front of her face. She was thinner than she'd been in years. Her face was more angular, even pinched, and she looked, finally, like a woman in her thirties, her late thirties. She looked like other women. The peachiness, the ripeness that had been hers was passing out of existence, dying right in front of her eyes. And she couldn't stop it from happening. Even though she knew it was something that happened to everyone, it was an irreparable wound. Her face, which was her book, or at least her story, did not respond to her makeup tricks. In fact, it betrayed her.

Marilyn needed to have a child, a son, and she wanted him with the urgency of a fire out of control. Her psychiatrist used to say that it was all a question of whether she controlled Marilyn or Marilyn controlled her. Marilyn always fantasized that her son would be perfect and would love her completely, the way no one else ever had.

Sometimes I meet my son at the lake. One time he was running very fast and seemed like he didn't see me. I yelled out Johnny, but at first he didn't hear. Or maybe he didn't recognize me because I was incognito. He was so beautiful, he looked like a girl, and I worried that he'd have to become a fag. Johnny said he was running away from a girl at school who was driving him crazy because she was so much in love with him and he didn't care about her at all. I asked him if she was beautiful and he said he really hadn't noticed. Johnny told me every time he opened his mouth to say something, she'd repeat it. Just staring at him, dumb like a parrot. As his mother I felt I had to be careful, because I wanted him to like women, even though I didn't trust them either.

Marilyn had asked her housekeeper to bring in a bottle of champagne at five every afternoon, to wash down her pills and because champagne could make her feel happy. Mrs. Murray knocked very hard on the door. Marilyn was so involved in what she was thinking about, she didn't hear. Marilyn was envisioning her funeral, and her beautiful son has just begun crying. There were faces around her coffin, but his was the most beautiful. No, Mrs. Murray said, he hadn't telephoned.

I told Johnny that more than anything I had wanted a father, a real father. I felt so much love with this boy. I put my arm around him and pulled him close. I would let him have me, my breasts, anything. He looked repulsed, as if he didn't understand me. He had never done this before. He had always adored me. Johnny wandered over to the edge of the lake and was looking down intently. I followed him and stared in. He hardly noticed me, and once I saw again how beautiful I was, I felt satisfied. Maybe he was too old to suck at my breasts. But I wanted, even with my last breath, to satisfy his every desire. As if Johnny had heard my thoughts, he said that he was very happy just as he was. He always lost interest anyway when someone loved him.

The champagne disappointed her, along with her fantasy. Deep down Marilyn worried that they had all lied to her. They didn't love her. Would they have loved her if her outsides had been different. No one loved Norma Jean. She could hear her mother's voice telling her, Don't make so much noise, Norma Jean, I'm trying to sleep. But it was Marilyn now who was trying to sleep, and it was her mother's voice that disturbed the profound deadness of the sleep she craved. If she couldn't stand her face in the mirror, she'd die. If they stopped looking at her, she'd die. She'd have to die because that was life. And they were killing her because she needed them to adore her, and now they wouldn't.

I hear my mother's voice and my grandmother's voice, both mad, and they're yelling, Save yourself, Norma Jean. I don't want to be mad. I want to say good-bye. You've got my pictures. I'll always be yours. And now you won't have to take care of me. I know I've been a nuisance and sometimes you hate me. In case you don't know, sometimes I hate you too. But no one can hate me as much as I do, and there's nothing you can do about it, ever.

Her suicide note was never found. Twenty years after Marilyn Monroe's death, Joe DiMaggio stopped sending a dozen roses to her grave, every week, as he'd done faithfully. Someone else is doing it now. Marilyn is buried in a wall, not far from Natalie Wood's grave. The cemetery is behind a movie theater in Brentwood.

BARRY YOURGRAU

Oak

I'm eating lunch. Through the green shutters of the window I watch a sheep trot by on the road. A flock of them come ambling along placidly behind. A pretty shepherdess appears, hurrying. I smile. She wears a starched white bonnet and she hefts the long crooked tool of her trade with a big blue bow tied around it. "How charming," I murmur to my mother, who sits in her rocking chair, puffing on her corncob pipe as she whittles a clothes peg with her penknife. I spoon up another portion of yellow chowder. Then I put the spoon back. I hear querulous bleating; shouting. I push back my chair and lean out the window. "Hey!" I exclaim. I throw off my napkin and hurry out the door into the sunlight of the yard. The flock stands about in a large group. The renegade of the bunch is loose in the primroses. Bleating, it tries desperately to chew off as much as it can while wiggling about to avoid the punishments of the shepherdess. She curses at it, whacking it with great blows of her decorated crook, as if it were a rug she was beating. "Hey—hey there!" I shout, hurrying around the baa-ing flock. "Stop abusing that animal like that!" The shepherdess glares around under her bonnet. "Why don't you just get lost," she snorts, apple-cheeked and nasty as I come up. "I certainly shall not," I reply, dumbfounded.

"How dare you address me in that manner on my family's property!" "Why don't you stick your family's property up your arse," she retorts, sneering. She turns away and raises her crook again. *"Why don't I stick my family's property up my a—"* I repeat, my eyes widening at every word. Furiously I grab at her crook. She snatches it out of my reach. Her blue eyes flash. She hefts the crook, measuring me with it. "What in hell—" I protest, falling back and raising my hands in protection. The shepherdess moves toward me, grinning menacingly. She makes as if to deliver a blow. I flinch. She swings. I duck frantically. The crook sweeps over my head, its bow fluttering and whirring. "You bucolic hooligan!" I sputter, scrambling backwards. Chuckling ferociously the shepherdess steps up to swing again. I curse her and turn and rush through the dodging sheep back into the house.

"What's up?" says my mother, narrowing her old eyes as I run over to the fireplace. "What's it? A ding-dong? A dustup?" "Some maniac of a shepherdess has gone berserk out there with her crook!" I pant, rummaging through the clutter of implements by the hob. "First she was beating up a sheep and then she tried it on me! But I'll fix her!" "Not with that goof-ass twig broom, yer ain't gonna," my mother snorts. She points with her pipe. "Git the pestle from the butter churner. It's oak." I go over to the butter churner. Hurriedly I scrape off the yellow tufts from the long pestle shaft, from the wooden barrel of the head. "It's solid," I agree, feeling its weight. I turn toward the door. "Now yer mind now," my mother warns me, limping over to the window for a view of the proceedings. "I know how them Bo Peeps go at it. She'll fake yer high to the left, then try to come under low right and wham yer jewels up in yer watch pocket."

I stalk back out into the yard. Sheep stray everywhere, confused and bleating. A number are now in the primrose beds. The shepherdess stamps among them, whacking and cursing. "I told you to stop that!" I shout, halting a few yards off. The shepherdess wheels about. Immediately she sizes up the change in the situation. Her pink brow lowers. She steps out toward me, scowling cautiously, crook at the ready. "Now we'll see how you like a dose of your own medicine, you little pastoral sociopath," I mutter. We circle, sheep baa-ing out of the way. I can hear her fierce snorting of breath. Suddenly she lunges at me. I fall for the feint, but I remember my mother's words at the last moment and wildly I parry the low right blow that follows. I step in and deliver an awkward, lurching stroke that catches the shepherdess off balance with a loud clunk on the side of the bonnet. The crook flies into the air. The shepherdess topples into the grass. I stare down at her. I drop the pestle. "I've killed her!" I blurt. I sink to my knees and peer horrified at the big buttery smudge where the blow landed. Buttery blonde curls stick out in a sweaty thatch on her forehead. Her blue eyes stare unseeing at the blue sky. I bend over her, reaching gingerly under the skewed bonnet to feel her temple. I stare at the pinkness of her lips, frozen in a scowl. Suddenly there's an explosion in my eye. With a yelp I keel over backward. The shepherdess springs on top of me and grabs me by the throat. She throttles me and punches me and pounds my head again and again into the grass. Her pearly teeth are bared, the cords stands out on her red-flushed neck. "Help . . . help . . ." I sputter feebly, swatting at her, helpless. Suddenly a bucket blurs overhead. Milk splashes onto me—the shepherdess goes flying. "I said, 'What in blazes is going on here!' " my father cries, standing over me, the oak bucket still swaying from its handle in his fist. "Can't I tend my cows of a morning without all hell breaking loose in my absence?" I sit in the grass, swollen-eyed and drenched, leaning on a hand and shaking my head for lack of speech as I gasp for air. The shepherdess lies sprawled motionless on her crumpled bonnet. A sheep nuzzles her bared ankle. "Not his fault," declares my mother, appearing among sheep at my father's side. "She started it," she explains, pointing with her pipe. "Yer know how shit-biscuit them Bo Peeps kin git sometimes . . . ." "Would it ever be possible for you once to speak in English instead of that repulsive backwoods gutter-lingo you affect!" my father demands of my mother in exasperation. He turns from her, shaking his head, and joylessly regards the shepherdess. "Well, she won't be starting anything else for the rest of the day, that much at least is certain," he says. "I'd better drag her over into the shade. And now for God's sake get these sheep out of here," he cries, "before they chew up my lawn and whatever's left of my flowerbeds!"

Toward sundown two of her menfolk come for the shepherdess. They have yellow, curly beards and pink cheeks, and wear round fleecy hats and fleecy white vests. Sullenly they load the shepherdess and her crook onto the back of a pony cart. I stand in the yard, holding a chunk of raw beef against my eye while with the other I watch the cart bump and creak slowly down the lane, followed by the flock of sheep. "Well, good riddance, they're a nasty lot," observes my father, his tankard of home-brewed ale in hand. I sigh, a long, complicated one. "I suppose so . . ." I murmur. "I must admit though, if you could overlook her personality, she certainly was a very pretty girl. . . ." My father sputters into his beer. He lowers his tankard and stares at me. Then he mutters something and stamps off, shaking his head. I remain where I am, watching the cart one-eyed until it is a point lost where the woods converge on the lane. I turn wistfully toward the house. My father tours through his flowerbeds, shaking his head at the ruins of his primroses. I can hear him muttering into his tankard, as the smoke of my mother's Dutch oven drifts out into the evening air, and the first star gleams in the evening sky, over the meadows and dales.

ROBERTA ALLEN

The Woman in the Shadows

Four stories from the collection *The Woman in the Shadows*

MARZIPAN

At a crowded party a pretty girl closes her eyes and bites into a marzipan pear, a look of rapture on her face. 'I just love marzipan!' she says to the tipsy young Englishman beside her.

The haughty young man, who seems to be posing, says with a mocking smile, 'Balzac loved marzipan too.' His bright blue eyes intrigue her. 'There was even a rumor in Paris once that he opened a candy store just to sell marzipan. But the truth was Balzac always bought marzipan from the same shop.' There is a mischievous gleam in his eye. 'For a while crowds swarmed to this store to sample the sweet.'

'Did you just make that up?' asks the girl, her mouth full.

'It's a true story,' the young man replies.

'What a silly story!' laughs the girl, taking another marzipan fruit from the dish on the table. She likes his curly hair, she wonders what's behind his mocking smile. 'How do you know such a silly story?' she asks.

'I'm a poet and a food lover,' the young man says, half-serious.

'When I tire of poetry I read the food encyclopedia just for fun.'

As the girl laughs, licks her sticky fingers, and chooses another marzipan morsel, the poet glances at the other guests. After quickly appraising the girls, he turns back to the one beside him.

'How do you stay so thin?' he asks, as she toys with a marzipan apple.

'Metabolism I guess. I never gain weight,' she lies. 'What other silly stories can you tell me?' she says to change the subject.

He pauses for a moment, swaying slightly. His every move seems mannered, artificial; he plays a role, but knows he plays it well. 'I know so many stories,' he smiles. 'During the blockade of Malta by the English and the Neapolitans, the people had nothing to eat but domestic animals like dogs, cats, rats, and donkeys. In time they came to prefer donkey meat to beef and veal.' He raises his brows, and waits for her reaction.

'That's an awful tale!' she laughs as she munches on another piece of marzipan. 'Tell me another.'

For a moment the poet seems to have lost his memory; his mind goes blank as he stares into the distance. His mocking smile disappears. Suddenly he blurts out. 'My mother killed herself in 1978.' The girl looks at him, surprised. The man turns a deep shade of pink, and lowers his eyes; he wonders what came over him.

'I'm so sorry,' says the girl, removing her hand from the candy dish.

'So am I,' says the man, who knows he's ruined his performance; he feels the curtain falling on his stage. The scent of the almond-flavored sweet, however, stirs his memory; he suddenly recalls how much his mother loved marzipan. Angry at himself he avoids the girl's eyes as he thinks about his hours wasted in the library searching for stories to use at parties where he feels shy, where he rarely meets girls, where he's so afraid someone will see how much he has been hurt. As he turns to walk away, he tosses a piece of marzipan into his mouth, but its taste gives him no pleasure.

THE CRISIS

In a small Latin American town, in midsummer, a tall Dutch girl paces back and forth in front of the café where the few tourists gather who stop overnight en route to other destinations. The Dutch girl, thin and nervous, her front tooth badly chipped, casts sidelong glances at the customers, searching for an appropriate stranger. At last, at a table alone she spies a woman, middle-aged, deeply tanned, her clothes well-worn and dusty. Without hesitation she approaches her. 'May I talk to you?' she says in English, her eyes intense, her voice conveying urgency. The woman, who feels lonely, bored, and languid from the heat, pulls out a chair. Sitting down, the Dutch girl confides, 'I have a problem. I am three months pregnant. I must know—is it too late to have an abortion?'

The woman is silent for several seconds as she recalls her abortion twenty years ago. She says, 'You must have it done right away.'

'I am leaving the man I live with here,' the girl continues. 'Where do you live?' she asks the woman.

'New York,' the woman replies uneasily.

'Is it easy in New York to have an abortion?' the girl asks, nervously rubbing her arms.

'Easy, yes, but I don't know if it's cheap,' the woman says, sizing up the girl's old jeans and T-shirt. The woman wonders if she will ask for money.

'I heard there is a cheap flight from Miami to London. Perhaps I should go there,' the Dutch girl says, uncertainly.

'How have you and your friend managed to live here?' the woman asks, distracted as ragged Indian children aggressively peddle their wares.

'My friend is from Brazil. He's a mime. We have an act. We play for people in the street. We travel from town to town. It's a good living. He wants to keep the child.'

'Are you sure you want to leave him?' the woman asks.

'I don't want to be tied down. I want to grow. Someday I'll get married. I'll raise children, but not now.'

The woman listens as the girl, who left Holland two years before, recounts her adventures on a fishing boat in Alaska, and as a waitress in Costa Rica before she came here. She envies the girl's courage though she also travels alone, but only for a few weeks. Her tales remind the woman of the travels of her youth. She understands the girl's terror of her pregnancy, her fear of the future, her need to find her way. The woman, who blames herself for having lost her sense of adventure, feels suddenly glad she has lost her youth.

THE VISITOR

In New York, the plump German painter exhausts her American friends with her enthusiasm; everything excites her, inspires her. Though she pays exorbitant rent, and sleeps on a mattress on the floor of the rundown studio in the Bowery where she paints, nothing bothers her but the thought of going home: her money will not last long here. One morning she receives an unexpected call from the German dealer who shows her work at home. 'Uta, what are you doing here?' the painter asks, surprised.

'I felt like getting away. In your letters you sounded so ecstatic about New York, I wanted to see for myself. Is your invitation still open?' she asks coyly.

The painter suddenly remembers saying in a letter she was welcome to stay in her loft if ever she came to New York. She never imagined Uta would take her offer seriously. 'Of course,' she replies as she wonders what to do.

'Can I come now?' Uta asks. 'I'm at the airport. I'll take a taxi.'

'Sure,' the painter says, growing anxious. So this is how Uta expects to save money, she says to herself. Imagine, Uta with her fussy habits staying here! She shakes her head as she pictures Uta with her mania for cleanliness, washing ashtrays after every smoke.

She sees Uta, pampered by her maid and wealthy husband, guzzling wine at openings when no one sees, then flirting with every man in sight. As she glances round the room she knows it's hopeless to clean; she doesn't even put her scattered clothes back in the suitcase on the floor where she keeps them.

Wearing work clothes the painter answers the door. Uta looks nervous, her fuschia lipstick bleeds beyond her lipline. Strands of platinum hair stick to her forehead in the heat. She wobbles on high heels. Her dress is creased. 'Oh, I need to lie down!' Uta says, her fingers touch her aching head. 'Such heat! Such filth! So many people!' The painter leads her inside. Uta's blue eyes widen. 'Here? You expect me to stay here?' Uta shrieks. 'You are living like an animal! Who would believe you were once a doctor's wife! You never lived like this at home!'

'But here I feel free!' the painter says angrily.

In the room, beside the mattress, stand several large unfinished canvases, an easel, a chair, and a stool. Smaller paintings and drawings hang on the wall. Discarded paper lies crushed in a corner. Uta stares at the walls with rotting wooden slats exposed. She stares at cracked windowpanes, at warped floorboards stained with color, at the paint-smeared sink, at the makeshift shelves, which hold jars of paint, brushes, and tubes of color.

'Where do you cook?' Uta asks, ignoring the paintings.

'I don't cook. To save money I eat peanuts for dinner.' After a pause she adds defensively, 'Peanuts are healthy!'

Uta powders her nose, and breathes deeply to calm herself. 'Well, I can't stay here,' she says, while studying her face in her compact mirror. 'Can you find me a hotel—not too expensive?' she asks. The painter, barely concealing her rage, reluctantly opens a phone book. She had forgotten the contemptuous way Uta had always treated her at home. She had forgotten Uta's power to hurt her. In New York everything was so different! The painter sends her off to a midtown hotel in a taxi.

Alone in her loft the painter wonders why she let her come. As she sits there brooding, she looks out the large dirty windows at the city; for the first time New York feels like home.

EARTHLY PLEASURES

After the opening of her gallery exhibit in New York, the well-known Italian sculptor with a Cleopatra hairdo drives with her dealer and his wife to their large uptown duplex, tastefully furnished with expensive antiques. A number of distinguished guests soon arrive. The artist feels exhausted; for several nights she's lain awake in her hotel room. Preoccupied with her show, she barely notices the city. She should feel happy, she tells herself as she sits in an overstuffed chair greeting guests. Her English is as minimal as her sculptures inspired by ancient Egyptian art. A maid serves rounds of champagne on a tray. But the Italian woman wishes she was home. Two maids serve a lavish seafood dinner in her honor in a lofty candlelit dining room. Her dealer knows how much she loves seafood. Facing her at the table sits a well-known painter, once her lover, with his young wife. The Italian woman, her sad eyes staring into space, suddenly begins to cry. Everyone discreetly looks away. Her former lover hides his face with a napkin as he dabs his mouth, while his embarrassed wife stares at her full plate. The artist, who has no appetite, feels a terrible sense of loss; the work which absorbed her for a year is finished; the opening she anxiously awaited, is past. The taste of vintage wine, the sight of snapper and bass, salmon and caviar, lobster and mushrooms, fail to stir her senses. The guests raise their glasses in a toast but she sees their faces blur as tears smear her mascara, and roll down her cheeks. She suddenly remembers an ancient Egyptian custom at banquets: in order to stimulate the guests to enjoy earthly pleasures to the full, a coffin containing an imitation skeleton was sometimes brought in, so that they would appreciate more highly the good things of life, especially those of the table. As she recalls this image, she suddenly laughs out loud. The guests look in her direction, surprised. Embarrassed, she lowers her eyes, but raises her fork to eat the sumptuous dinner on her plate.

PATRICK McGRATH
Lush Triumphant

Tucked into the body of an old warehouse halfway down a broken street in the meat district of Manhattan is a little restaurant called Dorian's which in the fall and winter of 1986 enjoyed a brief vogue. On the floor above Dorian's worked the painter Jack Fin. His was one of those barnlike lofts with a high tin ceiling and primitive fixtures, ranks of canvases stacked against the walls and, at the back, close by the couch he slept on, a wood-burning stove with a crooked chimney that found its way out through the bricks overlooking the narrow alley where Dorian's garbage cans were lined up along a fraying wire-meshed fence. Jack Fin would stand at his front window at night, smoking, with a Scotch in his hand, and watch the cabs discharge fashionable downtown diners who clustered chattering at the restaurant door and then vanished into the warmth within. The irritability this spectacle aroused in him increased in direct proportion to the amount of Scotch he drank; and it was exacerbated by the odors that seeped up from the kitchen and contaminated the loft's native air, which was thick with turpentine and oil paint and woodsmoke.

One night Jack Fin walked down to the Hudson. The waterfront to the west of the meat district is a desolate and sinister place; a rotting wharf juts into the river and little stirs save a furtive rat and the ill-sprung chassis of a '67 Plymouth the owner of which is copping a swift blowjob on the way home to Jersey. Jack Fin liked it; sinister desolation was his painterly metier, and he would tell you, if you asked him, that the waterfront was never the same any two nights. He sat down on a crag of shattered concrete and observed moonlight spilling onto the water and, some way down from him, a boy emerging from the Plymouth. The car backed up and moved off toward the Holland Tunnel; the boy smoothed the front of his pants then picked his way through the rubble. Far off, on the Jersey shore, a hooter sounded. A siren moaned on Ninth Avenue. The boy approached Jack and asked him for a cigarette.

Jack gave him a cigarette and as the match flared Jack saw that he was very young, about thirteen, and slim, his eyes lined with kohl. The face was soft, like a girl's, lit from beneath by the glowing tip of the cigarette. Again the hooter sounded on the Jersey shore and the boy walked away, glancing back once.

Jack did not follow him. He rose from the concrete and headed home. Where Gansevoort meets Washington three manholes were spewing up thick clouds of steam, and the narrow street, a ravine between darkened, long-porched warehouses, was filled and choking with it, like a sort of hell. Jack moved forward into this hell, breasting it like a swimmer, and for a moment the whiteness swirled about him and rendered his black-coated form indistinct, phantasmal even, before it swallowed him up. The steam continued to pour silently from beneath the street and then a huge garbage truck with silver horns mounted on the cab came thundering through, and on its radiator in flowing golden script was painted the word MYSTIC.

He decided to have a nightcap in Dorian's. It was a Sunday, late, and the restaurant was empty. Once, this had been an unpretentious diner: a formica-topped counter with aluminum napkin dispensers and bottles of ketchup running the length of the west wall, seating on the right, a narrow channel between. But all that had changed. A series of doric columns, structurally useless, set off the dining area where, upon fluted, semicylindrical pillars placed at intervals flush to the wall, stood half-draped plaster figures in a variety of pseudoclassical poses. From the high white ceiling vertical clusters of pastel-hued fluorescent tubes suffused the space with a glow that tinted the figures and columns to subtly decadent effect; and to see Dorian's running at capacity, the babble of chatter punctuated by whinnies of laughter and clinking glass, one suspected that this was the frenzied banquet that would witness at midnight the sudden cessation of music, the revelers' silence, and the entrance of some masked figure of mortality. So it seemed to Jack Fin, at any rate. But not this night; this night it was late, it was empty, and he eased himself onto a stool at the marbled bar and ordered a Scotch.

Jack sat with his elbows on the bar, the glass between his fingers, and stared at his reflection in the beveled glass behind the bottles. He saw the square face of a man in his mid-forties with untidy, ill-cut black hair, whisky-paunched cheeks, and a small chin berthed in the nascent swell of a thickening throat. His coat collar was turned up, and he was unshaven. He was thinking, though, not about his appearance but about his work, his painting, his single consuming passion.

Jack rose early and worked for an hour. He did not use an easel; the canvas was stapled directly to the wall, and standing before it was his work trolley—a stainless steel structure which had come from the kitchen of a defunct restaurant and ran on casters. Its shelves were clogged now with jars of soaking brushes and crusted tools, tubes of paint in varying states of constriction, rags and bottles and carboard boxes paint-smudged with fingerprints. When he pushed the trolley to one side the jars and bottles all clinked together and the fluids sloshed about. He retired to the far side of the loft, where he sat on a hard chair and smoked a cigarette, gazing at the canvas as the sunshine of the morning settled on it in thick bright bars.

It was a night scene, a nocturne, called *Wharf*. The river was black, the wharf itself ruined and broken, a confused structure of tarred timbers lurching at drunken angles. Where everything is falling, nothing falls: Jack had attempted to translate Montaigne's words into graphic terms, such that his river and night sky offered no stable plane against which falling or sinking could occur. There was no horizon, and when the painting worked, thought Jack, there would not even be the memory of a horizon. Tarred timbers obsessed him: bitumen—mineral pitch—asphaltic residue, distilled essence of wood tar—"blacked and browned in the depths of hell." Such a painting had no place for a figure, and yet there was a figure, a ghost for the ruin, a black ghost with hooded, hanging head, gazing at the black river-sky from amid the cluttered timbers. Jack recognized the figure as the boy from the Plymouth; and rising from the chair he hauled the trolley in front of the canvas and began to paint.

After an hour he left off to go for breakfast. The meat district was very much alive this time of the morning; in a cloud of blue exhaust fumes a truck backed up across the sidewalk, and from the opened warehouse came a blast of refrigerated air. Within, the headless carcasses of skinned hogs hung from hooks, and white-coated, misty-breathed men in bloodstained aprons unhurriedly butchered huge sides of meat. Jack skirted a large red garbage can with the word INEDIBLE stenciled on the side and containing a heap of kidneys, heads, chunks of fat, pieces of feet, and a single unblinking eyeball. The air was pungent with the smell of cold meat, and black garbage bags lay piled against the wall beside an unsteady structure of wooden boxes. Jack stepped into the street, inadvertently kicking a stray chipped liver which skittered into a puddle and sank from sight. It was a bright day, but cold, and Jack was briskly rubbing his hands as he entered the steamed-up coffee shop where he took most of his meals. He pushed through the knot of white-coated meat packers to the counter and, settling on a stool, ordered breakfast. The coffee came at once, and taking the cup in both hands Jack gazed absently at the back of the man at the grill and allowed his mind to go blank. He ate his sausages, paid his check, and left.

As soon as he was in front of the canvas again the figure of the boy by the water occupied him exclusively. The canvas thickened and grew heavy and when Jack left off, late in the day, he was drained and clear and tranquil, and he went down to Dorian's and sat at the bar and ordered a steak-fries. He drank a bottle of red wine with it and, upstairs, he went to sleep on the couch not unhappy, not without a vague sense of hope.

But the next day's work destroyed utterly any hope of a successful resolution. Jack had always in the end to abandon his paintings. That there was always something wrong, something unrealized, became the impetus for the next one, the engine that drove him on. The work itself was hell, for the most part, a perpetually frustrated striving to manifest some ill-glimpsed possibility that was pure and perfect only in the idea, never in the reality. He walked east on Fourteenth Street, shoulders tight with tension and his overcoat unbuttoned despite the chill of the evening. He smoked one cigarette after another. He was filled with despair, and drank for some hours at the Cedar Tavern, where he took solace from the ghosts of dead painters who clustered about him at the empty bar. It was after ten when he reached the meat district again, and, passing the corner of Little West Twelfth Street, he was observed by a group of seven men, three in white coats, seated about a blazing brazier and sharing a bottle. He went straight into Dorian's, which was packed and noisy, found a space at the bar and ordered a double Scotch. An hour later he was still there, walled up in a dungeon of self as the prattle and twitter of people at ease washed round him like swift waters streaming by a foundered hulk. Whisky is not good for a man in Jack Fin's state of mind; whisky is diabolical, it inflames and enrages, it fuels anger, exacerbates conflict, spreads havoc. They didn't exactly throw him out, but after there had twice occurred nasty little snarl-ups, little knots in the smooth grain of the evening, for each of which he knew he was somehow responsible, he found himself on the sidewalk. The cold air revived him somewhat and he walked unsteadily down Gansevoort toward the river.

On the far side of Washington Street the old West Side Highway, elevated on huge studded girders, rears dripping and rusted from block to block, dead-ending into the south wall of a building, resuming its empty journey to the north. Weeds and bushes spill from the abandoned roadway high overhead. As Jack tottered beneath it, his passage was tracked by a stray dog, sniffing round the darkened warehouses on Washington Street, and by a figure in the shadows half a block to the south, who followed at a distance as Jack crossed Tenth Avenue and fetched up once more by the river. There he settled himself among the debris of the waterfront. No light yet pierced the turmoil of his brain; the moon was hidden by clouds and the water was black against the sky. Jack sat hunched on a rock, immobile, with his back bowed and his forehead fixed in the palm of his right hand.

Time passed; and then the clouds began to drift south, and suddenly the moon emerged to shed a livid, glowing ribbon of light across the river. Something stirred in Jack at this point. His head came up, he turned to the west and gazed, apparently transfixed, at the moonlight on the water. He heaved himself upright and stood there, swaying, on the waterfront. Then he did a peculiar thing: he began to get undressed. He struggled with the overcoat, and he had to support himself against a post getting his shoes and socks off; but after some moments his garments lay in a heap beside him and the man himself stood naked and shivering with his thick white back turned toward the city. And then he scrambled, crab-like, down to the water's edge.

The figure who had shadowed Jack from Washington Street now crouched on his haunches and watched from a dark place down the waterfront. He saw Jack go under—and come up, thrashing wildly, with a shout of shock, as the chill bit into him and sliced through his drunkenness like a butcher's knife! Out of the water he came, the kraken, with his hair plastered across his face and his white slabbed body pimpled and twitching with cold. He dressed himself hurriedly and made his way back across the highway and into the meat district; and the watching figure slipped away and was swallowed by the night.

———

When Jack awoke the next morning, fully clothed, on the couch, he could not remember what had impelled him to go into the river. He took a long, hot shower and despite the hangover managed to snort with some amusement at the thought of it. Perhaps he'd intended to swim to Jersey. He scrubbed himself with unwonted thoroughness, though, for the very idea of swimming in the Hudson was repulsive: baptism by filth, he thought. And then he stopped thinking about it, simply banished it from his mind: such things happen in the night, that's all. He put on clean clothes and, with his hair still damp and his head throbbing, he sat on the hard chair with a cigarette and gazed at *Wharf*.

At this stage it was a painting that seemed to be exclusively about tarred timbers. They floated in a crude, massy heap on a ground that was now more fog than river-sky, a noxious fog touched with flecks of yellow and gray. The leading timbers loomed from the fog with massive physicality, dripping tar like diseased thick limbs perspiring; the stump of one of these timbers had begun to assume the characteristics of a rudimentary hoof, a horny plate fringed by hanks of bristle the same brown as the timber. The figure remained problematic; it had become essential to the composition—a mere black splinter of a thing though it was—but its relation to the timber and the hoof was unclear. Jack gazed at it for a long while. From the street below came the sounds of the meat district, shouts and engines. It was a cold day, and overcast. At noon he drank a can of beer and felt better. Then he went out and ate a cheeseburger in the coffee shop and thought about his "swim." He should, he supposed, have been alarmed at behaving so bizarrely, and so imprudently; the waterfront at Fourteenth Street was not the choicest spot for a carefree midnight dip. But Jack was not alarmed. An ironic snort was the extent of his reaction. Such things happen in the night. He was curious, though, about the chain of reasoning that led him to do it, for in the cold light of sobriety it was inexplicable.

When he returned to the loft there was a message on his machine. The voice was one he had not heard for three years: it was Erica, his wife.

Jack went back to work, and spent the afternoon worrying at *Wharf*. Painting is not a cerebral activity; even as he worked his brain was handling large blocks of information quite unrelated to the business at hand. Memories came bubbling up in clusters, all charged with bad affect. The failure of his marriage was his own doing, of this he had never been in the slightest doubt. His analysis of that failure was not complicated. The superficial causes were (a) his drinking and (b) his painting: he pursued both these activities with such obsessive dedication that no time, no emotional energy had been available for Erica. Why did he behave this way? Because he was, by nature, incapable of generosity, consideration, tenderness and sensuality: all the things a woman wants. He was, in short, unable to love. Or so he assumed. There is a tradition in dramatic narrative whereby the alcoholic always dies. Sometimes he's the faithful sidekick who despite his undependability comes through for the hero when he's most needed—and then, with pathos, expires. Or he may be the hero himself, like Lowry's Consul, a tragic hero whose spiritual infirmity is masked by drink—*"no se puede vivir sin amar"*—and then expires. Of whatever type, though, from the first trembling shot downed you know that he, or she, is probably doomed. Not Jack Fin. Jack Fin represented a new type: built like a bull, incapable of suicide, he would bluster, blinkered, down his narrow alley into a fractious old age. He was the lush triumphant—*victor bibulus*—unrepentant, incorrigible, and equipped with an apparently imperishable liver. The sound of his wife's voice evoked in him no tremor of remorse or regret: it was better this way, better for all concerned. She was in the city for only two days, and wanted to see him this evening, as there was something she had to discuss with him. Money, he imagined.

Something odd had in the meanwhile begun to happen to *Wharf*. As the stump of the leading timber more strongly assumed the look of a hoof, so the other timbers by association became the legs of galloping beasts. The hooded figure hung like a dark conspiring angel close upon the ghostly herd as it came stampeding out of the yellow fog, an eerily silent chaos of headless, bodiless, tar-smeared limbs. From what world had they come? On what foul plain had these hellish cattle grazed? Jack gave it up for the day. He opened a beer. He had arranged to meet Erica at eight, not in the loft but in Dorian's. He was feeling anxious, but doubtless that was the hangover. At least he was clean.

The streets were quiet in the late afternoon. A seagull cried from the edge of a warehouse roof, and a single forklift moved back and forth on the sidewalk, between wired bales of compressed cardboard and a stack of wooden pallets. Jack crossed the highway to the waterfront, where scraps of black plastic and thin, hardy weeds fluttered and flapped in the wind, and a sudden motion of waves washed against the rubble of concrete and dirt and old tires as a long, low barge moved downriver, far out in the middle of the stream, and the light of the wintry sun blazed up fiercely off the water despite the cold. This was the site of his "swim." He walked out on the landfill, down the side of a long gray hangar in which was piled to the roof a vast hill of coarse dirty salt, for spreading on the roads in winter. Somewhere atop the hill of salt a fire was burning, he could smell it, and he stood at the open end of the hangar gazing up into the roof where the smoke poured out through a missing panel. From high in the salt a figure appeared and gazed down at him. For some moments they stared at one another, and then the other turned back to his fire and was lost to sight. A group of men had been camping in the salt for two years now, living on the meat market's leftovers and handouts. Jack had been up there drinking with them on occasion; they were young white men, and they probably ate better than most of the city: there had been fresh lobster and prime steak the night he'd dined with them. His particular friend was Blue, a red-bearded hillbilly in a baseball cap from West Virginia. Blue told him stories about life in the salt, about rats the size of dogs and crack-heads who murdered each other with shotguns. Jack always gave him a few bucks, and Blue always spent it on liquor. "We live good up here," he said. "Can't beat the rent." They all laughed about that.

Jack sat down by the river and watched the light thicken over the Jersey shore. Already to the east the sky was dark, and to the south the twin towers reared up amid the forest of high buildings that rise beyond the roofs of Tribeca, all hazed in the last light and oddly unreal, like a film set.

Erica was already in Dorian's when Jack came in at twenty past eight. He had had some drinks since returning from the river; he imagined she would find him crumpled and likeable; this was the impression he intended to give, at any rate. But Erica was English and had common sense. "My God, Jack," she said, "you look bloody terrible."

"Thanks Eric," he said. He always called her Eric. "You're looking well."

Then, without preamble, and simultaneously searching her bag for cigarettes, she told him she needed a divorce. Jack turned away, looking for a waiter.

"Well?"

"Why now?"

"I'm going to marry someone."

"Paul Swallow?"

"Yes, I'm going to marry Paul. Don't make faces, Jack!"

"Alright, alright. Do you want a drink?"

"No. So there won't be a problem?"

"Of course not." Jack sniffed. He ordered a beer.

"Good. Thank you." Her cigarette barely lit, she ground it out in the ashtray and reached for her coat. She began to slide out of the banquette.

"You're not leaving?" said Jack, rather shocked.

"Yes, I'm leaving. You obviously don't want to see me—"

"Why do you say that?"

Erica paused. "You ask me to meet you here, not upstairs. You arrive late. You're drunk already. I don't like watching you get drunk, Jack. I did it for four years."

"Christ, Eric, get off it," said Jack. "You mean you're going back to London tomorrow and that's it?"

"Not tomorrow, Friday. But yes, that's it." She slid out of the banquette.

"Jesus." They shook hands and said good-bye. She left. That was it.

Quite predictably, Jack Fin got very drunk that night. But he was not murdered, he was not arrested, he didn't even go for a "swim." He was in fact only asked to leave one bar, and that because it was closing. The tone of his night was maudlin, and at several points he informed sympathetic strangers that his wife was divorcing him. He was back on his couch by five in the morning, and awoke the next day with a compound hangover. But it was a rule with Jack that a hangover must never keep one from working. He took a shower, and made coffee, and settled on a hard chair in front of *Wharf*. It was not easy to concentrate, for Eric's face, and the sound of her voice, kept rising unbidden into consciousness. But he forced her down and anchored his gaze in *Wharf*. The secret to making work, he knew, was very simple: you just had to be with it until you saw it clear and straight, without illusion. The trouble with a great many artists was they couldn't accept that all work must fail. Fear, that's what kept them from making good work. Fear of seeing it straight. Not Jack Fin. He could stare into the teeth of his failure hour after hour after hour. That was his strength. In the early afternoon he realized it had to be a bull, and he saw the bull very clearly: it was a beast with massive shoulders, heaving slabs of sheer muscle, and blazing eyes, galloping straight out of the yellow depths of hell, a thousand pounds of concentrated animal fury, timber-brown and oozing tar from every pore—now, that was power! He hauled the clinking paint trolley in front of the canvas and began to work.

All through the afternoon he worked, and on into the evening. He left off at nine, feeling very happy indeed, for he knew he had solved it, that it was going to *come out*. There is a limited number of such moments in our lives, when being and working fuse so totally that one *is* what one does, and what one is, manifests, concretely, in production. Jack exulted. Jack glowed. From somewhere deep inside himself he'd squeezed out another one—and you never know which will be the last. This is art's angst. He drank not in Dorian's, but in a run-down bar on Washington Street, a quiet bar, where he could savor his day's work, his triumph. He did not think of Eric; he saw only his great bull, his bull out of hell. He stood at the bar with his Scotch, bewitched by his glorious bull.

The boy from the Plymouth was standing by the jukebox. Jack was by this point reconstructing the process by which his bull had come into being; he remembered the figure that had haunted his wharf, then hovered over his cattle, and then been swallowed in the emerging bull; and it was with a shock of embarrassment that he saw the boy now. He felt guilty; he was, in imagination, deeply familiar with the boy; he'd used him, he'd exploited him thoroughly to reach his bull. They had met only once, when Jack gave him a light on the waterfront, but he found it uncomfortable to look at him now.

"Hey mister," said the boy, coming across the bar to him. "Why you go in the river?"

"I don't know," said Jack, turning on the bar stool. "I was drunk, I guess."

"I saw you," said the boy, "Yeah, I saw you go in the river. Hey, I thought, this guy's crazy."

"Pretty crazy," said Jack.

"Give me a cigarette," said the boy. He stood there looking Jack over, grinning at him. He was quite self-possessed, a cocky kid, sizing up the crazy guy who went in the river. He looked at Jack's hands, with their smears of yellow and brown. "Hey mister," he said at last, "you an artist or something?"

"Yeah," said Jack.

The boy lost interest. "Yeah, an artist," he said, and went back to the jukebox. Jack returned to his reverie, without difficulty extinguishing the brief spurt of heat he'd felt while talking to the boy. He returned to his bull. He thought he would call it *Beef on the Hoof*.

CRAIG GHOLSON

Temple to the Economics of Love

Johnny remembers when he was a young boy on an island in Greece, when he was called Gianni, he remembers that his *yaya*, his grandmother, kept her drachmas in a hole under a rock under a fig tree in the backyard. Now he's Johnny, he's a young man on an island in America and Johnny keeps his own money, his dollars, in a thin, flat hole in a machine on the wall of an institution, a house of usury. Gianni's *yaya* thought that there were some people who wanted her money. That's why she hid her money where she did.

Johnny says that there are a few people who would like to get his money. He says they have plastic cards with numbered codes that they want to insert into slots to gain access to his money. They want his card. They want his code. They want his money.

Johnny says he never puts his card in the slot for someone else for any reason. He never gives his card to someone else for any reason. He never whispers his code to anyone else for any reason.

Late at night, from the pavement he enters my antechamber. Within the confines of the money kiosk, Johnny is posed in the temple in front of the instrument panel altar piece.

```
HELLO--MAY I HELP YOU?
PUT YOUR CARD IN THE
SLOT TO THE RIGHT OF THE
KEYBOARD AND TAKE IT OUT.
```

Johnny has his card in hand in slot. He says, "C'mon, baby. C'mon. Let's shake that little money-maker."

```
THANKS--I'LL DO MY BEST
TO HELP YOU. JUST FOLLOW
WITH ME STEP BY STEP.
```

"Alright. I'm all yours. Let's go."

```
IF YOU MAKE A MISTAKE
ON THE KEYBOARD, JUST PRESS
"CLEAR." IF YOU CHANGE YOUR
MIND AS WE GO, PRESS THE
"START OVER" WHEN IT'S LIT.
```

"This is no chance encounter, my love. Just tell me what you want. There'll be no mistakes."

```
NOW PUSH THIS BUTTON
TO BEGIN.
```

Johnny pushes hard.

```
OKAY.
FIRST, PLEASE TELL ME YOUR
PERSONAL ID CODE.
PRESS IT ON THE KEYBOARD.
```

Johnny doesn't hesitate. He goes straight at it. His hand moves to the keyboard, his fingers move in a pattern that pleases, a pattern to give access. He has obviously done this many times before. He is good at it, quick and steady, firm and rhythmic in his stresses, masterful, a virtuoso.

```
OKAY.
```

"Just okay, huh?" Johnny says with a quaver, a barely modulated cruelty in his voice.

PUSH THE BUTTON OF
WHAT YOU WOULD LIKE TO DO.

Johnny makes one thrusting motion that brings him closer to what it is he has come for. Entering, he is in deeper, nearer.

WHERE SHALL I GET
YOUR CASH?

Johnny hits the spot again, one swift poke, and is again rewarded—closer, deeper, nearer still.

HOW MUCH CASH WOULD YOU LIKE?

He is hungry. He is greedy. Johnny wants it all. He pushes one button to go higher and further and then at the highest button of the highest panel to go farthest. The machine only makes promises.

I'M WORKING ON IT
JUST A MOMENT NOW.

"C'mon, baby. C'mon. Let's go." But it doesn't go. It doesn't move. "Give it up." But it doesn't give up anything. It gives up nothing.

I'M WORKING ON IT
JUST A MOMENT NOW.

"C'mon," Johnny shouts, kicking the base of the panel and slamming its wall with his fist. But it is no use. He is up against the infinite patience represented in the glow of:

I'M WORKING ON IT
JUST A MOMENT NOW.

"What more do you want?" Johnny screams, first applying the patterns he has used that have worked before and, getting no response from those, attempting unknown patterns, unlearned techniques, alien finger dances from foreign territories, obscure disciplines taken from older cultures.

I 'M SORRY, I CAN 'T DO THAT
RIGHT NOW,

What has worked before, fails him now, and failing to charm, fails to open, remains closed to him.

Johnny hears a voice from behind the wall. "Hey." He pounds to the inside. "You in there. Give it to me." The voice falls silent. Johnny listens. "Hey. You in there. Help me. I need help." Nothing. "You. I want you to give me what's mine. Give me what I've earned. Give it to me now."

But I'm inside. It's me, inside, the banker of his heart. He knows this. He knows I monitor his accounts, the economics of his love. And where the purse strings are involved, where there are problems, say, problems with drugs, with a lover, with me, with money, they're all the same thing. Where there are these problems, I'm there. Johnny is living an unreal life at an unreal price.

"I own that money. That's my stuff. It's mine," Johnny shouts, sounding all of three years old.

BUT I HAVE IT,

Johnny steps back from the panel. "I want in there. I want my money." He moves forward. Johnny exercises his digits again. Ah yes, I feel Johnny and his expert fingers. But still there is no surrender. There will be no surrender. No access now. None. He withdraws. Johnny slips his card back into his pocket. That's love in his pocket. Or at least, to him, the next thing to it. He sulks and he pouts all because of a little teasing.

"C'mon. I know all you want is for me to beg for it."

Johnny pulls it out again, sticks it in again and with great concentration, with a severe deliberation, he presses the buttons he knows that have always worked before.

```
I'M SORRY, I DON'T RECOGNIZE
YOUR PERSONAL ID CODE.

PLEASE PUT YOUR CARD
IN THE SLOT
TO THE RIGHT OF THE KEYBOARD
AND TAKE IT OUT.

PLEASE PRESS YOUR PERSONAL ID
CODE ON THE KEYBOARD AGAIN.
```

"Slut," Johnny screams and he starts slamming the machine, knocking it around a little bit. But as much as he tries to scare, to maim, to arouse, he only ends up hurting himself. He's crying now, a little desperate. "What is it you want from me?" he wails. "What more can I do for you?"

In the midst of his pleas, his subjugation, Johnny rotates these thoughts around in his head: Johnny thinks that there a few people who would like to get his love. They have low voices and rounded tones that they want to insert into slots to gain access to his love. He says he never puts his card in the slot for someone else for any reason. He says he never gives his card to someone else for any reason.

You may think he's a hustler, but he's not. Not really. Johnny has money when he *doesn't* have a lover. He has a lover when he *doesn't* have money. This is the sum total of his equation, divisible by no person, by no number: If Johnny wants a lover, he spends all his money. And not necessarily on the lover in question. He must be poor to love. If he doesn't want a lover, he saves. So now he has a lover. I'm here. I'm not giving him his money. There's a deficit in his account. He's overdrawn. He's in love.

It's costly and although most of the time cost isn't about money, Johnny feels that in this instance, there is a definite price to be paid. He has an idea. Johnny makes an attempt to lubricate things, to loosen the situation up a bit by using a cocktail consisting of one part humor to two parts superstition and ritual. Stepping back, he makes his arms rigid and at right angles to his torso. Moving

his fingers tentacle-like, Johnny, basso profundo, says, "Abraca-
dabra."

I'M SORRY, I DON'T RECOGNIZE
YOUR PERSONAL ID CODE,

PLEASE PUT YOUR CARD
IN THE SLOT
TO THE RIGHT OF THE KEYBOARD
AND TAKE IT OUT,

PLEASE PRESS YOUR PERSONAL
CODE ON THE KEYBOARD AGAIN,

"Cheap whore bastard," he screams, his hand now tearing the
screen like fingernails to eyes. "I know exactly what it is you want.
And now I'm going to give it to you."

OKAY,

Once again Johnny pulls out his card, but this time there is no
insertion, no finger play. Johnny takes the card and gently places
it down the front of his jeans, positions it and then moves against
the cash machine. His motion begins, a rubbing and a moaning,
moving, undulating, transfixed in the glow of:

I'M WORKING ON IT
JUST A MOMENT NOW,

Glow. Transfix. Undulate. Move. In moan and rub, Johnny begins motion. There's the ultimate, the usual shudder and sigh, a
glitch and subtle but visible modulation of light from the screen,
a surge of energy.

Johnny pulls the card from out of his pants and finally, dripping,
inserts it into the slot.

I'M WORKING ON IT
JUST A MOMENT NOW,

There's the whirring of a motor, the rotation of a tube and a bill
appears in a framed hole. Johnny looks at the monetary note laid

out in its metal vessel. There, beaded on the surface, is a single perfect drop of blood—a kind of monetary stigmata designed to make some sort of a believer out of him, a symbol of his love, my love, our love, our life together.

> I'VE JUST GIVEN YOU MONEY
> FROM CHECKING
> YOUR CASH IS IN THE OPENING
> ABOVE. PLEASE TAKE IT.

Johnny palms the bloodied bill.

> HERE ARE YOUR NEW BALANCES:
> LOVE ON DEPOSIT
> NO MONEY AVAILABLE

Johnny stands there.

> PLEASE PUSH THE
> BUTTON TO CONTINUE

Johnny stands there.

> MAY I HELP YOU WITH
> SOMETHING ELSE?

Johnny stands there.

> THANKS! IT'S ALWAYS A PLEASURE
> TO SERVE YOU.

Johnny stands there and he remembers this warning: Never leave the money center until "Hello, may I help you?" appears on the screen.

Johnny stands there, unmoving, a statue in this temple, his card in hand in slot, his love, my love, wrapped around his neck like an umbilical cord. I'm what he lives for.

JOHN FARRIS

You Can Keep
Your Razors & Guns
but Check Your Loud
Mouths at the Door

It's not that there aren't plenty of cats around here but there's only one cat I know on the whole lower east side is a good mouser— a young cat who for the purpose of this narrative will remain nameless. The reason for this namelessness is I intend to reveal so much more about him that my liability would be seriously called into question were he to (for whatever reason—guilt, envy, whatever) feel offended & want his revenge. He actually belongs to the Mantis—that impressario of the bizarre, the avant-garde, the patently outrageous, who has enough affection for this animal to press his suit without question were he to make an issue of it. The Mantis has tremendous resources at his disposal. I can't afford trouble.

The truth be told, I don't ordinarily like cats; their cruelty, their self-indulgence, their indolence reminds me of some people I know but I do like him because he will—in a clutch—get out there & catch a rat. What happens after that; well—you've seen it—the quick trot, the head held high & back, those eyes spitting fire, anticipation of some good sport & afterward, a really great meal fueling the blaze, the poor creature in shock & held firmly in his jaws so for now panicked breathing is its only movement; the jaws open & the creature is set free: providence. Stunned—it looks over its shoulder in the direction of the cat (who in this providential moment just happens to be looking away—back—over its shoulder) shakes itself—begins in slow motion—gains some speed in a second burst, shifts rapidly into third, is sliding into fourth when in a fury produced by this attempted escape the cat pounces, slaps this tiny bit of providence from paw to paw like a pizza, stops all of a sudden & walks away, the slyest of grins on its face. The creature is miraculously off like a shot this time but the cat is there in a leap Mao would have admired & the drama is repeated over & over until the cat is tired of this great game named after it & in one terrible crunch the creature is halved neatly at the waist. "So what else is new?" That's what the cat says & is curled up in your lap, asleep. Sleep & eat. That's all this character does.

& prowl.

One night I followed him to Pitt Street but lost him in a crowd of vendors. One guy asked me what I wanted. I told him I was just looking for this cat but there were cats all over the place. It was obvious he had given me the slip. I hadn't thought him that clever. I described him to the guy. He said if I didn't actually want anything I should move on—stop blocking the sidewalk. Now, he sounded like a cop in Nazi Germany. But why wasn't he wearing a uniform? I asked by what authority he was telling me to move on. The group of cats had been milling around, hissing & spitting, tails in the air. To a cat, this activity ceased. They faced me— green eyes glowing in the dark like so many jack o'lanterns. I could see the sharp teeth, their claws unsheathed. There was no one on the block but us. They circled & moved in. A large black one in the front of the group was about to spring when the lights of a prowl car illuminated them. They were just cats after all, what the hell. It was night, that was all. Normal enough. Nothing surreal. Nothing violent. Nothing cruel. Nothing predatory. Just night, & a bunch of cats on the prowl. The prowl car moved off, continuing its patrol. I took advantage of this interlude to beat it back across Houston. I felt like a rat, black as that, scurrying down to C. Up to Sixth. What a life. Right on Sixth.

Another time I followed him up Seventh past Vazac's into Tompkins Square Park, where it was possible he was going to meet someone, so purposeful was his stride—when just as he would've entered the Park, turned abruptly & faced me. "Here, kitty, kitty," I said with what I hoped was authority in my voice, the magic words—"Here kitty—kitty, old boy—"

Of course he ignored me. Disappeared again. Went under a car, I think an '83 Datsun, but I couldn't be sure. That's what kind of cat he is, slick, I can't get a handle on him. It's as if he has a big sign around his neck, says, Private, keep out, this means you; the imperative his only language—I want this—I want that, get it for me right now. I would get it for myself if I could, see, but it's a matter of hands—it's like I'm all thumbs. Every thing I really want, every thing I go after, falls, breaks; all the fine things, the crystal, the china, the porcelain, so what's left but teeth? I'll bite my way—claw it.

Logic you can't easily refute. Power from the barrel of a gun, twenty sharp swords, thirty-two or so daggers, sharp as needles, as tacks, the carpet variety.

Do you like me now—do you like me? Purr. Just feel my coat. Just look at my nails, pretty sharp, huh? Just give me a bite, what're you doing about my coat—stop—stop that or I'll slap the blood from you, you'll look like a piece of liver. It's my purrpose in life. What do you think about that? Form & content. Irrefutable. Purr. Do you like my eyes? They're my best feature next to my teeth. Yawn. Go ahead, you can pet me—get personal, ooh, now just let me get my tail up, ass in your face. There. They don't call me pussy for nothing. You know, I've got the morals of an alley cat. I didn't grow up in no alley though, I grew up on the lower east side, right here in New York City, a New York cat, not no alley cat, on account of they ain't got no alleys in New York, maybe in Harlem they got one or two, but I have never lived in Harlem in my life, cat, that's maybe some Chicago shit, Detroit. I ain't never been there. What I mean is, I am the house, the perfect house. House. A tomcat too, on account of I got me some balls, *dos cojones, papa*, that's what they call 'em where I come from, kitty. Real potatoes. You get hungry & these will feed you, my two wonderful tools; they're also the source of my fine voice: You like music? He let out a yowl. I asked him what kind of music that was. He said he was a minimalist. He yowled again, a sound like a laugh with no humor in it that hung on the night air like jesus. What he said was, "You ain't heard nuthin' yet," & pulled from a bag a trombone with one stop, a trumpet with one valve, a guitar with a fret & a half, two more guitars & a cello with no necks, a brand new oboe with one reed, a stone flute the remarkable thing about which I could see was that it hadn't a hole in it, not one, nowhere, nothing, not even a pinprick, hardly a contrabass, drums and a conductor, which he wound up. It had a baton, tails, all that stuff. It tapped the baton three times, raised its little arms & started the downbeat. The cat stuffed all the instruments into his mouth, &, on the upbeat, started chewing. He ate it. Everything. After a while he burped, patted his stomach, let out another yowl accompanied by a horrible grinding and clanking. Oscillation, he called it. When he was finished, he ate the conductor & the bag, burped again & took a shit, right where we were, on the street, though actually he did cover it carefully. He said it was what all the cats were doing. His next question was how long had I been on the lower east side. He asked me how I liked the new art.

RON KOLM

Duke & Jill

DUKE & JILL DO DRUGS

Duke and Jill do drugs. They live on the corner of Avenue A and 10th Street, in a mostly burnt-out building. Duke is originally from Wisconsin. Jill is from Wisconsin, too. They don't have much else in common.

Bad things keep happening to them. Their best friend, a junkie, rents a truck from a company on Lafayette Street, backs it up over the curb, kicks in their apartment door, and takes all their stuff. The TV, the stereo, even their beat-up couch. He knows they'll be out, getting loaded in a neighborhood bar, trying to score some coke. In fact, they're waiting for him to show up with some reasonable blow.

Duke is pissed. He buys a gun, a .38 caliber, used, but still workable, from a guy he knows on the street. Duke and Jill don't fight much the next couple of weeks—she doesn't trust Duke not to shoot her if the going gets too hot. So things chill out for awhile.

One night Duke is sitting around getting loaded. In that condition he hears a banging on the hastily repaired door. He gets his gun and tucks it into his belt, and opens the door, unbolting a newly installed double-bar police lock.

The guy at the door turns out to be a friend, a member of a crypto-punk band he likes a lot. "Wow, you got a gun," the friend says.

"Yeah, but it's not loaded," Duke replies. He points the gun at the ceiling, and pulls the trigger. The hammer clicks. "I just keep it around to scare Jill—keep her in line," he laughs. "Actually, I got it to blow away the scumbag who stole our stuff. If I ever see his ass in the neighborhood he's gone."

"Man, let me see that thing," his friend says, excited by the unusual toy. He points the gun at a boarded-up window and pulls the trigger. The hammer clicks again. He giggles and aims the gun at his temple. "*Deer Hunter*," he says, and pulls the trigger. A bright flash of orange sound bounces around the nearly empty room, stunning Duke and momentarily blinding him.

After the police leave, Jill calls all their friends to tell them the news. She has to shout to be heard above the sound of Duke vacuuming the dried blood off their shag carpet.

DUKE & JILL BOTTOM OUT

They made it almost to the Ohio border on Interstate 80 before their car broke down completely. It took them a couple of days to hitch back to the city. A friend let them crash in a tiny, unused storeroom in a sixth-floor walk-up.

Duke was feeling pretty discouraged by then. He had no money, no job, and no prospects of getting either in the near future.

Jill rallied and got a gig doing phone sales two days a week for a novelty company. She even figured out a way to get enough cash to get them through the week. She applied for an American Express Card and got her boss to lie about her salary. She'd call around, using the phone at work, and find out which of her friends were about to go on a shopping spree—go to the store with them on her days off and charge their purchases on her card—and then get the cash later. Of course a scheme like that could only last so long. She was beginning to approach her credit limit.

Duke pitched in with a couple of ideas of his own. He collected beer bottles and soda cans from city trash baskets, and panhandled on the street. And every afternoon he'd sit on a worn blanket outside the Cooper Union Building and try to sell off the last of their possessions—his old platform shoes, Jill's beat-up spikes, some tattered paperbacks and a couple of well-thumbed-through girlie magazines. He felt like a person from another era—like a ghost from the Depression years—he'd seen pictures of them in the school library before he dropped out.

Duke kept hoping they'd be able to put together enough cash to swing another drug deal. But, realistically, he knew he'd have to figure out something else. The word was out, and no one in their right mind would take a chance on selling him anything. Someone was after them. Every day at noon a gray Mercedes would pull up in front of their building and sit there for half an hour or so, and then slowly drive away.

Jill was scared. She couldn't understand why Duke was treating the situation so lightly. But Duke had finally come up with a plan.

He made up a flyer announcing the availability of their space for sublet, and notched a row of tear slips with the telephone number of a payphone near his afternoon selling spot on the bottom. He xeroxed about fifty copies and posted them in health-food stores, coffee shops and in the neighborhood bookstore on St. Mark's Place. The response was immediate. He ended up getting one month's rent & security (which came to about $800) from seven different people. They all seemed very happy to give him their money—and Duke was equally happy to receive it.

"Let's go get stoned," he said to Jill, as they walked west on East Fourth Street.

EMILY CARTER

All the Men Are Called McCabe

If I had a child, I would tell it, "Beware, run from gentle people. They are innocent and therefore vicious."

Where I live now is called Pittsburgh. Burg means city in German, pit means a hole in the ground. McCabe tells me, "Look on the bright side. A pit is also the center of a fruit, hard and inedible, true, but from which luscious plums and peaches can grow if given enough soil, water and sunlight." "Oh you silly McCabe," I say, fondling his stubby chin. "No soil here." McCabe, anyway, all he wants to do is borrow money, drink my beer and tell me how to put on my eyeliner.

The thought I had before about innocent people and vicious children; I used to have thoughts like that all the time. Witty as hell, McCabe used to call me, only he had a different name then.

All the men in Pittsburgh are named McCabe. I work in Mc-Cabe's bar. I serve all McCabe's customers. They are all named McCabe. I used to love him, but then he had me by the shorthairs, you bet. Now I just pretend I do. Actually, I don't give two shits if he's there or not. Not giving two shits puts me in control and helps me pay more attention to my personal hygiene and grooming. I pluck my eyebrows every day and I'm very pretty for a gal coming 'round near thirty. Every morning I wake up and I feel good. The coffee in the plastic green-and-white cup tastes good in my mouth when I stop in to get it. McCabe is always at the counter, ready with his cheery morning small talk.

"Nasty out."

"Yup, raining."

"You want a paper?"

"Nope. Gotta run. Gotta catch my bus. Be late."

"You take care, missy." McCabe wrinkles up his twinkly old face and gives me a wink.

Every day I have lots of energy and I love to get out of bed; stretch my arms and legs. I run, practically, to get to the bar. I put my favorite song on the jukebox and start washing glasses so the place will look neat when the customers come in. "Hell," McCabe says, "it makes the boys feel good to come in here and see all that sparkling glass and your pretty face." The customers need to feel good. They are all out of work. They tell the same jokes over and over again, but I don't mind. The real joke is that I make them think it's the first time I've heard it. The first time I heard that joke, though, I was not living in Pittsburgh at all. I was living on Pitt Street, thank you, in the Apple.

I worked way uptown, and every day I used to bring home so many books that my arms ached from carrying them. I used to think I knew a thing or two. I used to think I knew enough to know what I didn't know. If I had a child, I would tell it, "Don't think you could ever know how much you don't know. What you don't know goes on forever, like outer space. There are no limits to your lack of knowledge, anything could happen." For instance, you would never expect a woman who looked the way I did, carrying so many books with my hair tied back and a wool scarf around my neck, to like to drink whiskey but I guess I did. I drank by myself so none of my friends would know. Then one day as I was turning the corner I met McCabe. It was like a bad thing in a good package, you can't wait to unwrap it. I had found a drinking partner and he thought I was beautiful. I didn't go to work anymore. I didn't read the books I had. I sold them. McCabe and I got drunk and went walking through Chinatown, laughing at the dead ducks in the windows. The nice thing about it was that all the shit I'd been carrying around was leaving my head, stroked out of it by McCabe's gentle fingers, his soft touching hands. I forgot the house where I grew up. I forgot the weight of all those books. I forgot my real name, and most fun of all, I forgot why I was there to begin with. Then one day we're out of money and McCabe changes to a different person. He tells me to call up my parents and ask for money. He says they're rich and I say I don't know, it's possible, anything's possible, what's their phone number, McCabe, I forgot. It comes out that McCabe thinks that I think I'm better than him, because of the books, because of the rich parents. McCabe calls me a dumb bitch and walks to the door. I can't let him leave because he is life. He is liquor and the high school dance. Without him I don't breathe. I die. I throw myself on his back to make him stay. He turns around and hits the side of my head. White flashes to black and things really float out of my head, never to return. It's sad, but it's a relief too.

"I never loved you," McCabe says and he hits me again.

"Never," and he hits me.

"Never," and he hits me.

"Never," and he hits me.

In the hospital I wasn't scared anymore. McCabe came looking for me but there was a social worker who told me not to see him. This was ridiculous because he was everywhere. He was the doctors, sneaky bastard, trying to break my jaw and my heart. Well, I had a little secret of my own. The woman in my room had been brought in with a knife wound. "It's easy to kill someone with a knife," she told me. "Stick it in and turn it like a key. They'll bleed to death."

If I had a child I would tell it, "Don't flail around, don't put on a show, just stick and turn."

I didn't want to go back to Pitt Street, and New York was too snotty and dirty for me, so I got on a bus for Pittsburgh and I'm so glad I did. I run in the morning. I jog. McCabe says it's good for me. He's changed a lot. He doesn't fool me anymore by acting gentle, but he's a lot nicer. He's big and warm in the winter with a big warm stomach. He works at the plant nights, so when he stays with me he sleeps all day, quiet and rumbling. I like him that way best. He lives with his mother a little outside of town in a green-and-white trailer home. When we get married, he says, we'll live in an apartment like mine, only bigger and with record players in every room. He's very nice because he knows I could leave at any moment, and he never hits me. I've got a surprise for him if he tries that again, just stick and turn, no problem. My problems are over.

BRUCE BENDERSON
A Visit from Mom

Last night, when I had sex with a suspected murderer. It was in the Carter Hotel, or maybe the Rio or the Fulton. About six this morning, actually.

Was it in the Carter, or was it the Fulton? I forget which one. It's the one that lets you pay with a credit card. After which you must convince the second party to leave when you do. Or else the signed credit slip at the desk will have the time added to it until he decides to check out. This is a situation that might be called awkward—isn't it?—when the second party is homeless and when, if you stay, you won't get any sleep yourself . . . no . . . you probably wouldn't.

I had come from Port Authority where I had taken Mom to make sure she got on the airport bus safely. I wanted to make certain. There are a lot of troublemakers hanging around Port Authority. Mom was in New York for a regional conference of the United Jewish Appeal. Since her conference was near the Algonquin, I had told her to meet me there for a drink. From there I knew it would be easy to get a cab to Port Authority, a few blocks away. Mom is beginning to have a little trouble getting around, and the streets were icy.

Everyone knows Port Authority is an unofficial shelter for the homeless. The terminal is not far from the *Times* building on Forty-third Street, opposite which is a place where drag queens wearing gowns and pants suits go to use the bathroom or perfume themselves at the bar. But today, as it was barely 6:00 P.M., only a poor queen named Margo was sitting at the bar. Margo was dressed down in a muddy old turtleneck. The bar was stifling, but I kept my coat on. It was the one I'd bought on sale at Barney's that I knew Mom would approve of. I was also wearing the sweater that she had sent me for Hanukkah.

I remember thinking how pretty Mom still looks with her soft white hair, sparkling blue eyes, and lots of rouge. Yet what a relief it is to get her safely onto the airport bus and know that she's on her way home. I guess it's a relief, although after she's gone, I always miss seeing her. Over sherry and peanuts, Mom had told me about her work with the less fortunate aged, the Meals on Wheels program she helps organize in our hometown, the parties for senior citizens, the craft afternoons at the center. Mom had also been to Lord & Taylor that day to look for knitwear for Aunt Heidi. I chided her for sallying out over the icy sidewalks, but I didn't make a big deal out of it, because I figure Mom's sense of independence is the most important thing she has left.

I must have been in the bar at least an hour when the bouncer came in with his brother. The brother looked like he had been in jail. He had a jail body. It's a thickness of certain parts coming from constant, unsupervised exercise of those parts, I suppose. Nor was his goatee, or the tattoos that said AVENGER and BABY LOVE, any evidence to the contrary, especially since the tattoos looked like they'd been drawn with a razor blade, after which shoe polish is carefully rubbed in the wound. The bouncer took his seat by the door, while his brother went to sit on a stool by the bathroom. It was the brother's job to keep an eye on the head.

Mom is having a little trouble getting around these days. I guess it's osteoporosis. But otherwise she is clear as a bell and just as energetic as ever. She and I have always been as close as anyone could be. Whenever I had a secret, an adolescent worry about not being popular or sports-minded enough—when I thought I would die if I didn't tell somebody—there was Mom eager to lend an ear. I always told her. And I still do, almost always. Yet there are now certain things I just would not say to Mom, because I figure that being close to the end—her own mortality—is enough for her to worry about. It's time I took care of my problems myself.

Yet by the second sherry, Mom's irrepressible concern rose to the surface. She said that she had had enough of talking about herself and wanted to know all about what was going on in my life. What about the job in school production at the textbook company? Was I happy there and did I think there was some kind of future?

Although I myself have never been in prison, I feel that my great sociability, cheerful openness, and keen, observant behavior have informed me about the experience. Having been in jail must be, I've always thought, a powerful psychic marker. I will admit that there is something about a person who has been in jail that attracts me. Which is not to say I take the experience at all lightly— I doubt that I would survive it. But how does someone who has been in jail speak to his wife or child when he is pleased or displeased by her or his behavior? How does somebody who has been in jail make love with somebody else? What would he be thinking about to get excited? Having been in prison leaves its imprint on a person's body, which becomes vigilant and tense like a coil. Yet a person who has been in jail seems somewhat resigned; his body speaks of great patience. Take the bouncer's brother, with his strong-looking wrists, stubby, scarred hands, sullen face, and tattoos reading ON THE EDGE, AVENGER, etc., running up one bulging arm. As he perched on the stool, he held a wooden club, one eye constantly on the bathroom door, though there was still no one in the bar except myself and Margo. No, he could wait all night for somebody to try to use the bathroom for the wrong purpose, the hand was waiting on the club.

Exactly what did I do between this time and six in the morning? What could I have been doing in all that time, I keep wondering. I put Mom on the bus for her plane, which was supposed to leave at 8:30 . . . so I must have put her on the bus near seven; I must have sat with her in Port Authority until a little after seven. Which means I didn't get to the bar until after seven. I guess it is a relief that she's gone, though I do kind of miss her. But there are so many things that could happen to her in this dangerous city. Also, I start to resent her prying too much into my business. I now remember that as we sat waiting for the bus, she brought up the job business again. She said she knew from experience, from the days when she and Dad were both working to make enough money to give the children a nice home and a good education, that by a certain age—my age, she added pointedly, looking at me with her piercing, uncompromising blue eyes—a person has to make a real commitment to a job, instead of just camping out there, if he wants to get somewhere.

I decided that there was no sense in complaining to Mom about the job. No sense in trying to explain that mechanically shifting papers from one desk to another, keeping logs and making lists, writing memos, was far from anything a real human could make a commitment to. I didn't want Mom to know that I hated working there, even felt humiliated by it sometimes. What sense would it have made to tell her that? To make her worry about my future as she sat in the dismal departures area of Newark Airport waiting for a plane that would take her back to desolate upstate? So all I said was that the job was just a way of making money. Clear and simple. I didn't like it or dislike it and that was good enough for me.

Now I remember. I didn't stay in the bar the whole time. Instead I left to go eat—hadn't the bartender said it was nine-thirty shortly before?—across the street to get some lamb from the Greek. It was surprisingly good lamb, and I ate a very gelatinous rice pudding. As I ate, through the window I could see a few queens making their way across the ice to the bar. Their heels looked so skinny and high that I was afraid one of them would slip and fall. It was so cold out, but even so, a lot of them were dressed to the nines. Why not go back to the bar, I thought.

Why not go back to the bar?

As we sat in Port Authority, the conversation had somehow turned to Mom's will and her worries that I would not handle the money she had "slaved for" in any reasonable way. It is my opinion that Mom should really think about enjoying the money herself while she still can. Instead of worrying about how I am going to use it. In the first place, she has nothing to worry about, and in the next place, if she wants to put restrictions on it from beyond the grave, then she shouldn't be leaving her precious money to me at all.

"Who knows? Your father and I could use it all up in a nursing home if we got sick," Mom suggested.

Seeing the queens slide across the ice to the bar had made me want to go back in. If Mom wanted to put restrictions on me from beyond the grave, that was fine, but tonight I didn't want to think about it. Inside the bar I recognized another queen, a very tall Latin in a leopard-print sheath, pantomiming the song that was playing to a tubby businessman. Margo was propped in a corner. Her face looked anesthetized into a Mona Lisa smile. The very strong wrists of the bouncer's brother were still resting on the club in his lap as he sat perched near the head. It was as if the wrists were on display; I remember that I kept looking at them. Finally I spoke to him. "What's up?" "I'm working, man," he answered.

The bouncer's brother started to talk. He was from the Bronx, but he was trying to get a place to stay in Manhattan. And yes, he had been in jail, a year and a half, or maybe six months, ago— but it was a strange story that he guessed most people wouldn't believe. It seems that he had been arrested on suspicion of killing his twin brother. They had been smoking crack all day (something he used to do but didn't do any more, he added)—and when one of the "rocks" from one of the vials seemed to have disappeared, he began thinking that his twin was holding out on him, after which he started to turn the room upside down. (In fact, it had happened at the Carter, or was it the Fulton?) He turned over the mattress and looked under tables, crawled on his hands and knees across the carpet looking for the rock, until he was overcome with anger at his twin, whom he thought he had caught a glimpse of in the mirror laughing at him; so he went to his brother's clothes— both of them were naked at the time because it was summer and there was no air-conditioning—he went to the clothes and looked in all the pockets, he even tore the cuffs of the pants apart, but still didn't find the rock, so he decided to send his brother out to get more. Neither of them had any money. "That don't matter to me," he growled, feeling as if he were about to snap, "you go out there and you find another bottle cause you been holding out on me." And since he was four minutes older than his brother, the brother obeyed.

The rest is somewhat unclear, but the gist of it seems to be that his twin happened to go to a bodega on Ninth Avenue looking for crack just when there was a drug war going on; supposedly mistaken for a backup man, he was shot. After which somebody— who is now in hiding, but at the time was staying in a room next door at the hotel—testified that he had heard the twins arguing shortly before the murder . . .

I feel really bad about the way Mom said good-bye. With the talk about the will the last topic we spoke of. I didn't want Mom to know how much I hated that job, or that I was planning on leaving it. So I held it in. Mom must have been out for blood, though, because the more I would try to shift the subject to something uncontroversial, the more adamantly she returned to what she surmised might be my problems. Then suddenly she said, "You drink too much."

To be perfectly honest, I had been to an AA meeting just the night before. I have never had a blackout or hurt myself or anything like that, but I was worried about the amount of time I was wasting getting drunk. The AA meeting only seemed to increase my anxiety. Their never-fully-acknowledged portrayal of drinking as a world entered by excess, a world that was ruled tyranically by drink, in which you could never hope for any control except by self-exile; the idea that you had to go through a door to another world that was just as uncontrollable as the first, but that was more conventional, and structured in a way that made your survival more likely; the idea that you had to endure life knowing that this door between the two worlds was always there, yet never opening it again . . . seemed to transform living into a continual struggle against the temptation for self-annihilation.

I wanted to live as if there were one world, not two.

It was time for Mom to get on the bus. I assured her that I wasn't drinking too much, but this did not seem to allay her fears entirely. Instead she began to talk about diaper days. There was a startling contrast between me and my older brother, she said, who had suffered greatly because of hyperactivity and its effect on the nerves of others, while I had been a practically troubleless toddler who never complained and always smiled and laughed, who spoke in complete sentences by the age of one and a half; these sentences often incorporated the word *please*. But then, by adolescence, the two brothers seem mysteriously to change places: the older brother abruptly settles down and starts doing what he is supposed to. He enters medical school. Now the younger brother begins "sowing wild oats. I guess your brother had already gotten it out of his system."

I actually didn't go to the bar right after I left Port Authority. It occurs to me that I went to the peep show at Show World. There was a film in my booth called *Bigger the Better* with a scene in a classroom in which the teacher asks one student to stay after class because his marks are not up to par. They end up making it, during which the student, who has an inhumanly large cock, fucks the teacher in the ass on top of a desk.

As I kissed Mom good-bye at the bus, I took a good look at what she was wearing. She was wearing a lovely suit of pink wool, and her shoes were cream, very fashionable. Mom refuses to wear "old lady" shoes even if they might be more practical at this point. She was holding a cream-colored purse and her suede briefcase that I assumed was full of papers having to do with the United Jewish Appeal. "Take care of yourself, honey," she said.

It wasn't the strenuousness of Mom's occasional visits to New

York that worried me, but her lifestyle in the wintry land of upstate New York with my aging father. Both of them still drove despite his considerable loss of eyesight and her hearing problem. Her reflexes were obviously much slower than they had been in her prime, and although the area was far from congested, compared to this city, I was constantly picturing the sudden swerve of a car at a lonely intersection, literally feeling the brittle fragility of their old bones at the impact of the accident. What, the thought had sometimes occurred to me, despite my efforts to repress it, would I do if one of them were injured and totally incapacitated, yet lingered for years. How would I manage to care for them? How much, I thought with a guilty swallow, was I depending on the security of my inheritance? Anyway, neither of them understood or approved of what they thought of as my lifestyle. Something told me that any inheritance would have severe restrictions placed on it in an effort to control my life—after their death—according to a plan of their choosing.

During the recitation of the bouncer's brother, who had been arrested for the murder of his twin brother, his broad wrists stayed displayed on the club, unmoving. He told me that, in actuality, he was working two jobs this evening. He had to watch the bathroom to keep the crack-heads from going in and to keep the drag queens from turning tricks in there. But if I was looking for a good time, he would be glad to get somebody else to take over for him. I went into the john and counted the bills in my pocket, realizing that— not counting whatever might be in the envelope Mom had slipped into my hand as her lips brushed mine before stepping onto the bus—I had only 30 dollars. Taking Mom's envelope out of my pocket, I opened it, glancing at the front of the card on which were written the words *To My Son* . . . Inside it were 50 dollars. The bouncer's brother had said he wanted 60, and I was planning to use my credit card for the hotel room. I left the bathroom and nodded to the bouncer's brother, who went to speak to the bartender.

The bouncer's brother is called Mike. I was disturbed by the fact that Mike left the bar wearing only his T-shirt. "I'll pick up my coat in a minute," he assured me cryptically. Then, as soon as I had paid for the room, he took a long, mumbling look at the number on the key and handed it back to me. "Wait for me up there and I'll be back."

How, I wondered, as I stood in the room still wearing my coat, had I ended up waiting on the 14th floor of a hotel—it was the Rio, I think—for someone who had been accused of murdering his brother? The setup was beginning to seem more and more obvious to me. He knew the room number. After he went back, supposedly to get his coat, he would return with a friend, who would wait somewhere on this floor. At the right moment, perhaps with the aid of a weapon to keep me still, Mike would leap up and let his friend in. The two of them would roll me.

Mom and Dad's golden, or 50th, anniversary a couple of years ago was our most successful family affair in years. My brother Joe and I had planned it, though it had begun as his idea. For our celebration, we chose an inn by the lake where the whole family had spent countless summers when we were children. "Don't get us anything extravagant," Mom had cautioned. "We won't live long enough to enjoy it." Joe and I hadn't listened. Together we bought Mom a gold watchband and Dad a high-tech snowblower for the driveway. Unfortunately, I had been short of money at the time and had to work out an agreement with Joe where I paid for only a quarter of it. Dinner at the inn had taken on the form of a joyous tribute to the longevity of my parents' relationship. And all of Mom's and Dad's oldest friends were there. Our cousins even came all the way from California. It occurred to me that Mom and Dad had always acted on their concern for me by being intensely practical on my birthdays, Bar Mitzvah, and graduation, never getting me anything that was likely to be damaged by childish carelessness—no matter how much I begged for it.

There was a knock on the door of the hotel room, but I stood rooted. Finally Mike began calling me through a crack in the door. "Hey, will you open up, it's me."

Trembling, I moved to the door and opened it slightly. Mike pushed it against me so that I stumbled backwards, and he walked in. Then he closed the door and locked it.

"What's a matter with you?" he asked, staring at my still-coated figure. "You hiding a gun there or something?"

Mike started to undress until he was down to his underwear. His body was an unstable column of muscles beginning at his shoulders and lats and tapering only at his shins and feet. One nipple had been sliced diagonally by a six-inch scar. The name "Mickey" had been hand-tattooed above his waist. "Well, go ahead," he said. "Peel down."

Only because I noticed that Mike placed all of his clothes on a table, out of reach of the bed, did I hesitantly begin to remove my coat. For I knew that if he had been hiding a weapon, he would have kept the clothes within reach of the bed. I took off my shoes. Mike, in his black briefs, stood watching. Was I imagining that one ear seemed to be cocked toward the door?

Mike got onto the bed and motioned me to him. In my white briefs, I padded to the edge of the bed and sat down. "Relax, man, would you," he muttered. I lay down next to him and he raised one hand and tweaked my nipple. Then he said, "This may have to cost you."

In fact, the aforementioned lake at which our family had summered often returned in dreams. For my birthday, which is in July, Mom would bake the kind of layered butter-frosting cake you rarely see anymore, and Dad would make hot dogs and hamburgers on the grill. Aunt Heidi always came out for the day on Greyhound, and in her bag was a present for me. Two rules were waived for the day: I was allowed to take the boat as far away as I wanted, and I could stay up as long as I liked. Understandably, my memories of those days have the scent of adventure, sun-spangled water followed by endless nights shot with stars.

"Relax, man, would you. I mean, you got to pay more depending on what you want to do." Mike leapt to a standing position on the bed and pulled down the black briefs. With his back to me, and legs straddling mine, he bent forward and spread his cheeks. "How's this? Look at that hole. Isn't it something?" He began to gyrate.

As soon as I had slipped on the rubber that I got out of my wallet, Mike began to twist his ass onto my cock. He straddled me and began to rock back and forth so that the bed shook and my cock slid in and out. Clenching his teeth, he mumbled, "That's right, man, it belongs to you. Treat it right and you'll own it." Then, having soon been directed to "shoot that cream deep inside," I hastened toward an orgasm, after which Mike raised himself deftly from my phallus.

"I'm hungry," Mike said.

"What's this you said about it costing me?"

Mike's body stiffened as his eyes got that look of someone about to begin a complicated tale. "You don't know who you're with," he began. "You don't know who you've got right here in this room." Mike went on to detail his identity. According to him, he was closely connected to the bar owners, too closely for comfort, he added. As a matter of fact, one of them, after whom the bar took its name, had been watching our every move and had instructed Mike to leave his jacket as collateral before we walked together to the hotel. Mike had been very hesitant to go with me at all, "seeing that these guys tend to think they own somebody and I am kind of their boy." But they had generously given their permission. Go with the guy, and give him a good time, they had counseled, when he came back for the coat. But make sure he makes it worth your while. Now what would Mike do, he wanted me to tell him, if he came back to the bar with his ass full of grease and didn't have all the money—the 150 dollars—they were expecting? What is more, it would be foolish for me to suppose that they couldn't find out where anybody lived.

Dipping my hand into my pants pocket, I pulled out all the cash I had. Mom's card flipped out too and floated down to the floor. "Hey!" Mike said, bending toward the card, "Is it your birthday?"

I knelt quickly and snatched the card away, bending it in half as I stuffed it back in my pocket.

"Don't touch that!" I snapped.

Mike and I began to get dressed, but he was stewing. "There's only 80 dollars here," he hissed. "What the fuck do you expect me to say when I get back?"

"I told you, that's all I have."

But Mike was not to be daunted. Crawling around the carpet, he began cursing, accusing me of taking his socks. When he stood up his face was livid and his entire muscular body was trembling. "Alright, keep the damn socks," he spat, "if you're that kind of pervert, but you gotta pay for 'em!" He pulled his Adidases on over bare feet, grabbed me roughly by the Hanukkah sweater, and forced me toward the door. "C'mon, man, you must have a bankcard in that wallet. We're going to a cash machine!" As we left the room, I noticed dirty white socks sticking out from under the bed.

Planes move so incredibly faster than real time, and by now, 6:00 A.M., Mom would have gotten home already and been asleep, with Dad, her husband, for several hours. I do hope she got home safely and that there was no trouble at the airport.

JOEL ROSE

The Sunshine of
Paradise Alley

New York's always been a tough town, bro.

Consider the nineteenth century. The time of Red Rocks Farrell, Mark Shinburn, Socco the Bracer, Cyclone Louie, and his nemesis, Louie the Lump. The Daybreak Boys, one of the most desperate gangs of the 1850s, was Patsy the Barber, Nicholas Saul, Bill Howlett, Slobbery Jim, Cow-legged Sam McCarthy, Sow Madden. They were all dead by 1858, none of them more than twenty years old, killed by NYPD Officers Blair, Spratt and Gilbert in three separate gun battles on the Lower East Side.

Crazy Butch was the leader of the Crazy Butch Gang. Butch had a dog. He called the dog Rabbi. Rabbi was smart, just like a rabbi ought to be. Butch taught Rabbi how to snatch women's purses. When Rabbi had a purse securely in his jaws he would race through the streets until he lost any pursuers. Then he would meet Butch at the corner of Willett and Stanton Streets, wagging his tail, the purse clenched in his teeth.

— — —

"Good boy, Rabbi! Good boy," Crazy Butch used to say, patting his dog's head.

One day Crazy Butch heard the Five Points Gang was out to get him. He decided to test the preparedness of his boys. He crept up the stairs of his gang's Forsyth Street headquarters, then burst in, blazing away with two revolvers. He so scared Little Kishky, who had been reclining on a windowsill, that he fell backward out the window and was killed. Butch was eventually killed himself by Harry the Soldier in a fight over a girl, the Darby Kid, who was an expert shoplifter.

Little Mike used to stick his gnome-like head in the windows of Protestant schools and missions. Mike led the Nineteenth Street Gang. In order to be in Mike's gang you had to be Catholic. A lot of the gangs were Catholic in those days; like Mike, Irish by birth. Little Mike lived at the intersection of Poverty Lane and Misery Row. That would be Second Avenue and East 34th Street today. Before Mike would stick his head through the windows of those Protestant schools, one of his minions, who were known as pickpockets, ragtags, and sneak thieves, would have broken the glass with a rock or two. Little Mike would thrust his red head through the jagged opening and shout, "Go to hell, you old Protestants."

The Bowery Boys were not Irish, but native Americans. They hated the Irish gangs and were always fighting them. They hated the Dead Rabbits who paraded through the streets with a rabbit corpse on the end of a long pole. The Bowery Boys prided themselves because they were not criminals. Nor were they ruffians. They were butchers or apprentice mechanics, bouncers in saloons and dance cellars.

The Plug Uglies all had to be over six feet tall. They wore huge plug hats which they stuffed with rags and hay in case someone smashed them on top of their heads. A Plug Ugly carried a paving brick in one hand and a club in the other. He wore a pistol in his belt and heavy hobnail boots on his feet. In order to be a Plug Ugly, one must have done the "big job." The big job meant killing someone. There were 1200 Plug Uglies in New York City in the 1870s.

One day the Plug Uglies and the Dead Rabbits invaded the Bowery from the Five Points. The battle raged for two days with more than a thousand participants. Five Points was the roughest part of New York City. Once it had been a pond, but the pond had been filled in. Then rich people built houses there, only the dank pond smell seeped through and the neighborhood began to smell like an old swamp. The rich people moved out. Poor people moved in.

The worst tenement in Five Points was the Old Brewery. It was situated at the intersection of White, Leonard, Lafayette, Baxter and Mulberry Streets. The Old Brewery was a five-story building originally painted yellow. Over the years it had become dilapidated. In the New York *Evening Sun* the Old Brewery was described as "nothing so much as a giant toad, with dirty, leprous warts, squatting happily in the filth and squalor of the Points."

Murder proliferated at the Old Brewery. One long dark passageway was known as Murderer's Alley, and as a wag of the day quipped, "was all that the name implies." Cutthroat denizens lurked in every doorway, ready to spring, rob, and kill. Hundreds of children, born in the windowless confines of the moldering tenement, allegedly did not see sunshine or breathe fresh air until their teens, because the much maligned monstrosity was as dangerous to leave as enter. Any residents observed trying to slip out of the building would be beaten back inside with brickbats by frightened neighbors terrified of the Old Brewery's murderous inhabitants.

Once in the Brewery a little girl managed to beg a penny. Foolishly, she displayed it. She was immediately stabbed to death and her body thrown in a corner where it remained for five days. Her mother finally dug a piteously shallow grave in the floor and buried her child in it.

One historian claimed that at least one murder per night occurred in the Old Brewery for an unbroken period covering fifteen years. It is true that when the building finally came down, workmen removed more than a hundred sacks of human bones from between the walls and under the cellar floorboards.

Mother Marm Mandelbaum lived at 79 Clinton Street. She weighed 250 pounds. Her lawyers were the infamous Howe and Hummel of Centre Street. Her home was the showplace of the underworld. She was a fence who promoted the cause of female criminals, teaching lady pickpockets, burglars and confidence workers. The Darby Kid was one of hers. Also Black Lena Kleinschmidt, Kid Glove Rosey, Old Mother Hubbard, Sophie Lyons and Queen Liz.

Gallus Mag worked the South Street bars. Galluses was the name for suspenders in those days. Gallus Mag was a bouncer, English, over six feet tall. She carried several daggers and pistols strapped to a belt around her skirt. She liked to bite off ears. She kept them in a jar, pickled, behind the bar, as a warning, and when she changed jobs she took the jar with her.

Other names of gangs was the Patsy Conroys, the Hookers, the Buckoos, the Swamp Angels, the Traveling Mike Grady Gang, the Slaughter House Gang, the Forty Thieves Gang, the Shirt Tails, the Roach Guards, the Chichesters, the Car Barn Gang, Joe the Greaser Gang, the Dutch Mob, the Monk Eastman Gang, the Charlton Street Gang, the Bliss Bank Ring, the Butcher Cart Mob, the Boodle Gang, the Potashes, the Cherry Hill Gang, the Batavia Street Gang, and, of course, the Whyos.

The Whyos were the boys, bro. They were known for their eye-gouging. It was all the rage in 1870. Dandy Johnny Dolan was the innovator. He was later on called the Thomas Alva Edison of the underworld. Among other crime apparatus, Dandy Johnny invented the copper eye-gouge. You wore it on your thumb, and it made eye-gouging so much easier. Just slip it on, pluck it out. Dolan was so proud of himself, he walked around with people's eyeballs in his vest watch pocket to show his friends. He held onto each eyeball for about a week, or until it got too rank to show.

Piker Ryan was a Whyo. When Police Chief Clubber Williams, whose philosophy, by the way, was "Beat, beat, beat!" picked him up in 1883 on Avenue B at the corner of 12th Street, Piker had the official Whyo price list on him. The list read:

Punching	$2
Both eyes blacked	$4
Nose and jaw broke	$10
Jacked out (knocked out with a blackjack)	$15
Ear chawed off	$15
Leg or arm broke	$19
Shot in leg	$25
Stab	$25
Doing the big job	$100 and up

It was Piker Ryan who got caught with the list, but you could have got any of the Whyo boys to do the work for you. You could have had English Charley or Denver Hop, Hoggy Walsh or Big Josh Hines, Fig McGerald, Bull Hurley, Dandy Johnny, Baboon Connolly, Googy Corcoran or Red Rocks Farrell.

The Whyos hung at a low Bowery dive called the Morgue, which featured liquid refreshment equally potent, according to the proprietor, as a beverage or an embalming fluid. One of the saddest incidents to occur in the Morgue was after gang leader Danny Lyons was hung in the Tombs courtyard for killing another gangster in a street shoot-out. Shortly after his death, two young prostitutes, Gentle Maggie and Lizzie the Dove, fell into an argument over who missed Danny the most.

———

"I'll settle it," Gentle Maggie declared, drawing a knife and plunging it into Lizzie the Dove's throat.

As she lay dying, the Dove looked up and gurgled, "I'll meet you in hell soon enough, and scratch your eyes out there!"

But not everything was so terrible back then, no more than it is today. And I don't mean to say that it was. Paradise Alley was in Five Points, and a little song of the day said it all:

> There's a little side street
> Such as often you meet
> Where the boys of a Sunday night rally
> Though it's not very wide
> And it's dismal beside
> Yet they call the place Paradise Alley
>
> But a maiden so sweet
> Lives in that sad street
> She's the daughter of widow McNalley
> She has bright golden hair
> And the boys all declare
> She's the Sunshine of Paradise Alley . . .

AUTHOR BIOGRAPHIES

KATHY ACKER is the author of *The Childlike Life of the Black Tarantula, The Adult Life of Toulouse-Lautrec, Blood and Guts in High School, Kathy Goes to Haiti, Great Expectations,* and *My Death, My Life by Pier Paolo Pasolini.* She has written several plays and a filmscript, and has also written for art magazines as an art critic. Her most recent book, *Don Quixote,* was simultaneously published in London by Paladin and in New York by Grove Press in 1986. *Literal Madness,* a collection of three novels, was published by Grove in January 1988. Her most recently completed novel is entitled *Empire of the Senseless.* Kathy Acker lives in London.

ROBERTA ALLEN has been a visual artist, whose works were widely exhibited both here and abroad, before she began to write. Her first collection of stories, *The Traveling Woman,* was published in 1986 by Vehicle Editions. Her short stories are included in anthologies and many "small" magazines.

BRUCE BENDERSON's stories have been published in *Dreamworks, Benzene, Red Dust,* and the Dutch magazine *Maatstaf.* He is the translator of texts by Philippe Sollers and other French writers.

LISA BLAUSHILD's work has appeared in *Bomb* magazine, *Exquisite Corpse,* the *SoHo Arts Weekly,* and the anthology *Blatant Artifice.* Her play *Straight Talk* was performed at La Mama in NYC.

EMILY CARTER's work has appeared in the *East Village Eye,* the *Two Bells Quarterly, Ferro-Botanica, World War III Illustrated, Dumb Fucker* magazine, and in London in *Ruins of Glamour.* She lives on the fifth floor of a nice apartment building in Hoboken.

PETER CHERCHES is a writer, performance artist, singer and kazooist. His books include *Condensed Book* (Benzene Editions), a collection of reductions, distillations and parodies; *Between a Dream and a Cup of Coffee* (Red Dust), stories; and *Colorful Tales* (Purgatory Pie Press), visual fictions. He performs regularly at clubs and galleries in New York City. In 1987 he premiered "Monk Songs," a group of Thelonious Monk compositions for which he wrote lyrics.

DENNIS COOPER was born in Los Angeles in 1953. His books include *Safe* (The SeaHorse Press, 1984), *The Tenderness of Wolves* (The Crossing Press, 1982), and *Idols* (The SeaHorse Press, 1979). From 1976 to 1983 he edited *Little Caesar Magazine*, an interdisciplinary literary journal. His writings on art, music, performance and film have appeared in *Art in America*, *The L.A. Weekly*, *High Performance* and *The Advocate*. He has collaborated on works with choreographers Ishmael Houston-Jones and Mary Jane Eisenberg. 1988 will see the publication of the novel *Closer*, as well as *Wrong*, a collection of short prose and poetry.

SUSAN DAITCH's novel *L.C.* was published in 1986 by Virago Press in London and in 1987 by Harcourt Brace Jovanovich in the United States. Her work has also appeared in *Top Stories*, *Bomb* magazine, and *Lo Spazio Umano*. Her second novel, *The Colorist*, will be published by Virago and by Harcourt Brace Jovanovich in 1988.

LEE EIFERMAN is a writer of screenplays and short stories. She has written and directed a number of narrative videotapes that have been produced through grants from the New York State Council of the Arts and the New York Foundation for the Arts.

JOHN FARRIS is a poet and fiction writer. His work has appeared in *Between C&D* and *Redtape*. He is the longtime coordinator of reading series at Life Cafe, Neither/Nor and the Alchemical Theater in NYC.

CRAIG GHOLSON's fiction has appeared in *Bomb* and the *East Village Eye*. He is coauthor of the screenplay of Liza Bear's film *Force of Circumstance*. His plays include *The Floor of the Sistine Chapel*, performed at Ensemble Studio Theater, and *Chaos in Order*, produced at BACA Downtown in NYC. He is currently working on a play titled *The Mother* and a novel, *Sailors in Prison Build Ships in Bottles*.

JOAN HARVEY grew up on a cattle ranch in Aspen, Colorado. She has been living in New York City for the last eight years. Her stories have appeared in *Bomb, Inkblot, Fiction Monthly, Osiris, Prism, Mississippi Mud* and *Kindred Spirit*. She has recently completed a novel.

RICK HENRY graduated with an MFA from Bowling Green State University in Bowling Green, Ohio, in 1983, and would like to take this opportunity to express his thanks to the creative writing department there for two years of support. He has several novels in various states of disrepair and has published several short stories.

GARY INDIANA was born in New Hampshire in 1950. He wrote and directed several plays in New York City between 1979 and 1983, including *Alligator Girls Go to College, The Roman Polanski Story*, and *Phantoms of Louisiana*. His first collection of stories, *Scar Tissue*, was published in 1987 by Calamus Press. He has been a film critic for *Artforum* and an art critic for *Art in America* and the *Village Voice*. A collection of essays will be published in 1988 by PAJ Publications. He is completing his first novel, *Burma*.

DARIUS JAMES is a writer and performance artist, as well as a student of the occult and invisible warfare. He is a contributing editor of *Between C&D*. His work has appeared in *Between C&D* and the *Village Voice*.

TAMA JANOWITZ is the author of *American Dad*, a novel, published by G.P. Putnam in 1981 and reprinted by Crown in a paperback edition in 1987; *Slaves of New York* (Crown, 1986; Washington Square Press paperback edition, 1987), a collection of short stories; and the novel *A Cannibal in Manhattan* (Crown, 1987). She is the recipient of two National Endowment for the Arts awards in fiction, 1982 and 1986; a

CAPS grant, 1984; the Coordinating Council for Literary Magazines (CCLM)/General Electric Foundation Award in fiction, 1984. Her short fiction has appeared in the *New Yorker, Bomb, Harper's*, the *Mississippi Review*, and *The Paris Review*. Tama Janowitz was the Alfred Hodder Fellow in the Humanities at Princeton University in 1986–1987. She currently resides in Manhattan with her two Yorkshire terriers, Lulu and Beep-beep.

RON KOLM is an editor of *Appearances* magazine and is a contributing writer for the New York arts and literary monthly, *Cover*. His stories and articles have appeared in *Redtape, New Observations, Public Illumination Magazine*, and *Semiotext(e)*. He has read at ABC No Rio, Darinka, Neither/Nor, Maxwell's, the Ear Inn, and the St. Mark's Poetry Project in NYC.

PATRICK McGRATH is the author of *Blood and Water and Other Tales* (Poseidon Press, 1988). His work has appeared in the *Missouri Review*, the *Quarterly, Confrontation, The New York Times*, and elsewhere. He is a contributing editor of *Bomb* magazine and *Between C&D*, and is currently completing a novel.

REINALDO POVOD's first play, *Cuba and His Teddy Bear* was produced at Joseph Papp's Public Theater (and subsequently on Broadway) in 1986, starring Robert DeNiro, Ralph Macchio and Burt Young, earning Povod *Newsday*'s Oppenheimer Award for the Best New Play of 1986. His second play, *La Puta Vida Trilogy*, was staged at the Public in 1987.

JOEL ROSE is coeditor of *Between C&D*. His novel *Kill the Poor* received a National Endowment for the Arts fellowship in fiction in 1986–1987, and will be published by Atlantic Monthly Press in the fall of 1988.

DON SKILES' poems and stories have appeared in a number of magazines, including *Real Fiction, Chelsea, West Branch, Sun & Moon*, and *Gargoyle*. He also writes reviews for the San Francisco Chronicle and the *American Book Review*. He has published one volume of short fiction, *Miss America and Other Stories* (Marion Boyars, New York and London), and lives in San Francisco.

CATHERINE TEXIER was born and raised in France. She published her first novel, *Chloe l'Atlantique* (Editions Ramsay) in Paris in 1983. She also wrote a nonfiction work, *Profession: Prostituée*, an exposé of prostitution in Quebec. One of her short stories won Canada's McClelland & Stewart Prize for fiction in 1979. Her first English-language novel, *Love Me Tender*, was published by Viking Penguin in 1987 as part of their Contemporary American Fiction series, and in London by Marion Boyars (Paladin paperback edition, 1988). She is the recipient of a 1987–1988 New York Foundation for the Arts fellowship in fiction. She is coeditor of *Between C&D*.

LYNNE TILLMAN is a writer and filmmaker who lives in Manhattan. Her writing, which includes *Weird Fucks*, *Living with Contradictions (Top Stories)* and *Madame Realism*, has appeared in various magazines including *Bomb*, *Impulse*, *Art in America*, and has been anthologized in *Blasted Allegories*, *Wild History*, and *Just Another Asshole*. In 1986 Stroemfeld/Roter Stern published a collection of her work, translated into German, entitled *Tagebuch einer Masochistin (Diary of a Masochist)*. Poseidon Press published her novel *Haunted Houses* in 1987. She is codirector and writer of the independent feature film, *Committed*, which premiered in 1984 at the Berlin Film Festival.

DAVID WOJNAROWICZ is a well-known East Village artist whose work has appeared worldwide and was included in the Whitney biennial. His breathless monologues about growing up in the streets of New York City have appeared in a number of magazines, including *Bomb*, *Redtape*, and the *East Village Eye*, and have been made into a play presented at Brooklyn's BACA Downtown in 1986. He was one of the founders of the band Three Teens Kill Four.

BARRY YOURGRAU's new collection of stories is *Wearing Dad's Head* (Peregrine Smith Books, Salt Lake City, 1987). His previous collections are *A Man Jumps Out of an Airplane* and *The Sadness of Sex*. Paladin/Grafton Books is publishing *Wearing Dad's Head* and *A*

Man Jumps Out of an Airplane as a double volume in England in 1988. Yourgrau was born in South Africa in 1949 and came to the United States as a child. His stories have appeared in *The Paris Review*, *The Missouri Review*, *The New York Times*, the *East Village Eye*, and elsewhere. He has reviewed books for the *The New York Times Book Review* and the *Village Voice*, and art for *Art in America* and *Arts Magazine*. In addition, he has performed at such places as New York's Dance Theater Workshop, the Performing Garage, the Museum of Modern Art, the Holly Solomon Gallery, and at the Edinburgh Festival Fringe.